COUNTER CLOCKWISE

A YOUNG ADULT TIME TRAVEL ROMANCE

LEE STRAUSS

la
plume
PRESS

COUNTER CLOCKWISE

by Lee Strauss

(previously published under the names Elle Strauss and Elle Lee Strauss)

Copyright © 2015 Lee Strauss

Cover by Steven Novak

ISBN: 978-1-77409-445-7

ISBN: 9781927547687

COUNTER CLOCKWISE
(The Clockwise Collection #5)
by Lee Strauss

ONE

So what if he was going to Europe with his college basketball team without me? So what if the cheerleading squad and head cheerleader, Fiona Frias the Floozy, was going too? So what???

I stared hard at the text message from Nate Mackenzie, my hot boyfriend of one year, nine months and five days. My college-all-star-athlete-first-string-forward-for-the-Boston-University-Terriers-basketball-team boyfriend.

Nate: It's official! We're going to Spain!! It was a close call with some passport issues, but just got word we're all clear to go!

All those exclamation marks were like stakes in my heart. Spikes to my feet. I felt frozen on the spot in the middle of a busy hallway in Cambridge High. Bodies brushed by wafting stale air and teen sweat, but it wasn't enough to propel me. My heart weighed heavy like an anchor and a scratchy lump formed in my throat.

Nate had promised me all my firsts, but the one first he

could never give me was international travel. I couldn't fly. There was always the possibility that I could trip—swirl back in time—and it was best if my feet were firmly planted on the ground when that happened.

So he was going to Europe without me. Big deal. If I wanted Nate in my life (and I did!), I had to make some concessions. I couldn't tie him down, guilt him into not doing things just because I couldn't.

I forced myself to text him back.

Casey: That's great. The Terriers are great. You'll do great.

Nate: I'm glad you think it's GREAT.

Casey: Are the cheerleaders going too?

I winced as I pressed send, immediately wishing I could take it back. This was the crux of my issue with Nate going to Spain and we both knew it. Fiona Frias, college girl, long-legged, green-eyed, Latin beauty was in love with my boyfriend and she didn't try to keep it a secret. At all.

Despite Nate's reassurances, I felt completely insecure. Here I was, still in high school, while Nate was halfway through his degree. Of course other girls would notice him. Of course other girls would chase him. Girls who were more mature and experienced than I was. Unscrupulous girls.

Girl. It wasn't fair to group all girls together. Just one girl. Just one unscrupulous girl.

It only took one.

Nate didn't text back right away and I knew I upset him with the question. For him it was an issue of trust, and all my overt and obvious inquiries about Fiona made him believe I didn't trust him.

I did trust him. It was *her* I didn't trust.

My phone finally pinged with his response.

Nate: Yes.

Only one word. Only one word! Gah! That was all he had to say? Nothing to comfort me and calm my worries?

Casey: That's Great!

The bell rang and snapped me back to reality. Lucinda, my best friend who seriously deserved a medal for willingly wearing that moniker, poked my arm. "You're going to be late." Then, seeing my face, she asked, "What's wrong?"

"Nate's going to Spain. With *her*."

We started walking down the hall toward my creative writing class. Lucinda's history class was across the hall. She knew all about my worries over Fiona Frias and the impending team trip to Spain. She shot me a look of concern —or maybe it was pity—before saying, "I think you're boiling things down a little too low."

"Am I? Nate will need the self-control of a saint to resist her over there," I said. "For one thing, the drinking age is lower and well, a guy's power of resistance goes down with each drink, and it's a million miles and several time zones away. Fiona..."

"Casey!" Lucinda grabbed my arm and forced me to look down into her dark, worried gaze. "Nate loves you. He's not going to do anything with Fiona. You have to trust him."

"I know. You're right." I felt like an idiot. When did I turn into this crazy, jealous maniac?

I made it to my seat in Mr. Ryerson's creative writing class just as the bell rang. I folded my long limbs under the desk, brushed dark runaway curls off my face and took a deep breath. Lucinda was right. I was overreacting. I hid my phone under the desk and texted quickly before Mr. R confiscated my phone.

Casey: I really am happy for you. Promise to send me lots of pics.

Nate: Of course. I don't leave until next week. I'll see you tomorrow night.

Tomorrow was Friday, and Nate had promised to come to Cambridge until he had to leave for practice on Saturday afternoon. It wasn't a lot of time but it was better than nothing.

Casey: love you

Nate: ly2

I let out a breath of relief. We were okay.

Nate would be gone for two weeks. It wasn't like we saw a lot of each other now anyway. We both had school and homework and jobs. With texting and Facebook, it would be like he wasn't even gone.

Mr. Ryerson petted his thick graying mustache as he called the class to order. I loved this class. Writing was something I could do as a time traveler without too much worry. For the most part it was a job of solitude. I didn't have to worry about touching someone, skin-to-skin, and accidentally taking them back in time. Only four people knew about my "gift." Lucinda, who was the first unlucky person to go back with me and also how I learned about the skin to skin thing; Nate, who wasn't my boyfriend at the time and my brother Timothy, both of whom were also accidental traveling guests; and Samuel, a fellow traveler. The only other one I knew.

No, that wasn't true. There was that blond girl I met in

the convenience store one time. Adeline? I wondered what happened to her and if she had a good-looking boyfriend who was being chased by another older, prettier girl.

I wasn't sure what kind of living I could make as a writer, but this class offered unit studies in several fields: journalism, poetry, short stories, novels, memoirs (mine would sound like fiction!) and scriptwriting.

"The deadline for your deposit on the Hollywood trip is today," Mr. Ryerson said, eyeing me specifically. I'd signed up back in November with no intention of actually following through. I only wanted to avoid the inevitable questions as to why I didn't want to go. I *did* want to go, but the class was *flying*. What if I tripped while in midair? It would be disastrous.

I broke eye contact with Mr. Ryerson and stared resolutely at my desk. Mr. Ryerson continued, "We're joining a script-writing class with students from Hollywood High and we'll visit all the tourist traps. Bring your laptops. Leave your winter coats."

A cheer went up in the room. I slunk lower into my seat, once again awash with discouragement.

"Casey?" Mr. Ryerson called my name and I snapped to attention. He stood at my shoulder and I looked up, past his bushy mustache and into his squinty, concerned eyes. He leaned in and lowered his voice. "Are you having trouble coming up with the deposit?"

It was like I suddenly had bionic hearing and caught the sounds of the other twenty-eight students quieting and cocking their heads toward me. "Yeah," I whispered back. "I don't think I can go."

"It's possible the school could come up with a subsidy."

It was so quiet in the classroom, Mr. Ryerson's words echoed off the wall. My cheeks flushed with embarrassment. Now everyone thought my family had money problems. I squeaked out, "No, that's fine."

"You're a good writer, Casey." He dropped a paper on my desk with a big red A+ on the top. "I'd hate to see you miss out."

I spent the class period working on a short film script about a stupid contemporary boy who gets stuck in the civil war era and joins the Union Army (write what you know!). I couldn't resist checking my phone when the lunch bell rang. I got a new Instagram pic from FabulousFiona! It was a selfie. Her abundant bosom peeked out of her cheerleader uniform (some things just aren't handed out fairly!) A couple basketball players chatted in the background. I recognized one of the guys as Nate.

Her comment: "Too bad you can't come."

I gasped. Fiona Frias just made this personal! My thumbs went into high speed and I immediately forwarded the image to Nate.

Casey: This!!!

He didn't text back. Of course, he was busy playing basketball while Fiona jumped up and down on the sidelines in a short skirt and there was nothing, NOTHING, I could do about it.

The thought of her traveling to Spain with Nate (I know, it was with the basketball team, but SHE thought it was with Nate) made my blood boil. I had to be careful or I was going to stress myself back to 1863 and I really didn't feel like dealing with that right now. I stopped at the fountain and sipped cool water, long and hard.

Breathe, Casey.

Once my heartbeat was under control I leaned against the wall and wiped my face with my sleeve.

Maybe I couldn't go to Spain with Nate and maybe I couldn't stop Fiona from going with him, but I could control some things in my life. I walked resolutely back to my creative writing class. I had a checking account and an unused crumpled check in my purse. I'd written only a couple checks in my life, but I remembered how. I gripped my pen tightly as I wrote the date, the amount required for the deposit and then scribbled my signature at the bottom with a flourish. I swallowed hard. I was going to Hollywood.

TWO

I DIDN'T TELL LUCINDA. This should've been a big red flashing warning sign that I was about to do something colossally stupid because I told her everything, but the ball was rolling now and I couldn't stop it. Not true. I could go back to Ryerson tomorrow and ask for my deposit back, but I didn't want to, so the more accurate thing to say was the ball was rolling now and I didn't *want* to stop it.

Lucinda was my taxi driver when I couldn't get Tim or Nate to do it, because I couldn't drive. Just another thing on the increasingly long list of things I *couldn't* do.

Lucinda shot me a quick sideways glance. "What's wrong?"

I answered a little too quickly. "Nothing."

A *pwa* sound escaped her lips. "Casey, I can practically see the dark cloud cartoon stationed over your head. You're not still stewing about Nate and Fiona?"

"No! I'm not stewing about *Nate and Fiona* because

there is no Nate *and* Fiona! They're not a couple! We're a couple. It's Nate and Casey!"

"Whoa girl." Lucinda frowned and signaled before pulling over to the curb. I caught a glimpse of my reflection in the side-view mirror. My long dark curls were in need of a split-end exorcism, and my cheeks were red from my emotional and embarrassing irrational outburst.

Lucinda turned down the music pumping from her dashboard speakers and shook her straight dark fringe from her eyes. "What's really going on?"

"I'm going to Hollywood."

She scowled. "I thought you were only letting people believe you were going to Hollywood."

"Yeah, well now I'm really going. I paid my deposit today."

Lucinda's mouth dropped and her hands flew to her forehead. "You really are losing it."

"I'm not losing it, Lucinda. I'm finally seeing clearly."

"Clearly? You know they're flying, right?"

"I know."

"Thirty thousand feet is a long way to fall."

"I'm not going to fall. I'm going to sleep." I'd been thinking about this option for quite a while. Weeks really. "I never trip while sleeping. I just have to make sure I fall sound asleep on the plane."

Lucinda crossed her arms. "You've got it all worked out do you?"

I gave her a half-shrug. "Mom has sleeping pills left over from last summer when Tim was missing..."

"I still don't get why," Lucinda said.

"Yes you do."

"Because of Nate and Floosy? Really?"

"No." Sort of. "Because of me. I need my own life."

"Don't you want to be *alive* for that?"

"I'll *live* through it." I spoke so strongly, I almost convinced myself.

She huffed. "Does Nate know?"

I shook my head. "He's coming tomorrow night. I'll tell him then."

"He's going to freak out."

"I know." My stomach curled with nerves. I hated conflict. But this was something I had to do. For me.

Lucinda straightened in her seat, checked over her right shoulder while signaling, and started driving. After a minute, she said, "Sam Capone asked me out."

"Really?" I was glad for the change of subject. "See, I knew he liked you!"

Lucinda's lips tugged up into a grin, "I can't believe it. He's just so cute!"

Her joy was contagious and I couldn't help but smile back. After a string of heartbreaks, Lucinda deserved to be happy. I hoped Sam was as good of a guy as he seemed to be.

"What are you guys going to do?"

"Pizza and a movie tomorrow night." Her eyes darted my way. "We hadn't made plans, had we?"

We often got together on weekends when Nate was away for out-of-town games. "No, Nate's coming."

"Right. You already said that." She clucked. "Last weekend before the big AWAY game."

"I'm fine," was all I said.

Lucinda pulled into my drive. Her eyes crinkled with concern. "You're sure you're fine?"

I nodded as I got out. "I'm sure," I said with a plastic smile, though my nose might've grown a little.

I BROKE the news of my trip to Hollywood to my family over dinner. We weren't often all home at the same time, because of my parents' jobs and my brother's work and social schedule, but today I could kill all the birds with one reckless stone.

"Remember that class trip to Hollywood with my creative writing class?" I said after a bite of roasted chicken. "I paid the deposit today." I glanced up at my parents with an eager expression. "Mom, you signed the permission slip back in November."

My dad put his fork down. His latte-colored skin crinkled around probing dark eyes. "When is it?"

"Next week, Thursday to Sunday. The rest of the money is due this Monday."

"That's a great opportunity," my mom said. Her blond hair had grown a lot over the last year and she swept it over her shoulders as she considered me. "I'm excited for you. You'll have a great time!"

My brother Tim glared at me. "Are you crazy?"

"What?" I asked innocently, fluttering wide eyes.

He leaned toward me and spoke succinctly. "They're *flying* there."

"I know that."

I could see Mom watching us from the corner of my eye. "Are you afraid of flying, Casey?"

"Kind of."

Tim shook his head and rolled his eyes. Thanks to my

time-travel abilities and Tim's own stupidity, he was the only one in this room who truly understood the implications of this seemingly benign class trip. He'd taken needless risks last summer and would pay for that the rest of his life.

I continued to pick at my chicken and ate the rest of my peas and mashed potatoes. The conversation moved seamlessly from my trip to my parents' workdays. Dad managed other people's money from a tall office building in downtown Boston. Mom talked about her plans for the ritzy house on Mystic River in Arlington she was hired to design. Her business had done well over the last year and our kitchen had enjoyed a nice makeover as a result. We now had classic stainless-steel appliances, mixed dark and light wood cabinets and granite counter tops. A large ornate clock took up most of the wall that extended from the kitchen into the eating area. I watched the time, waiting for ten minutes to pass before asking to be excused. Mom didn't like us eating and running.

"I have a lot of homework to do," I explained, "and it's Tim's turn to clean up."

"All right," Mom said. I carried my dirty dishes to the kitchen, scraped my plate, and loaded the dishwasher before heading upstairs. Mom's voice filtered up behind me. "I think it will be good for her to go on the class trip." I smiled until she added, "She spends far too much time with Nate. She's too young to be so serious. She needs to spend more time with kids her own age."

I almost stumbled on the steps. Is that what she thought? A small pit snuggled up to the larger one already lodged in my stomach.

Twenty minutes later, I heard heavy, uneven footsteps

thundering up the stairs and I wasn't surprised when Tim appeared in my room. He shut the door behind him.

"Casey? What are you thinking?"

"Come on in," I said. "Thanks for knocking."

"Your door was open. Don't mess with me."

Tim's tall, gangly form hovered over my bed where I stretched out. I closed my laptop and stared up at him. "I need to do this. Just leave it alone."

Tim huffed. "And I thought I was the reckless one."

"I'm not being reckless." My voice sounded thin and wimpy.

"Oh? And what happens if you trip in midair? No cavalry will be able to save *you*."

"I'm going to sleep through the flight. I never trip when I'm sleeping, remember?"

Tim rubbed the barely-there scruff on his chin as he considered this. "You better make sure you knock yourself out good."

"I will. I promise."

Tim relaxed into my desk chair, stretching his injured leg out. "I still think this is a really bad idea."

"Noted."

"Who else is going with you?"

I hadn't taken a good look at the list. "Probably everyone in my class."

He huffed. "I hope there is someone strong enough to carry you off the plane."

Me too.

THREE

It was Friday night and I fussed over what to wear, which I usually never did. Nate and I were comfortable around each other; we didn't need to stress over our looks.

So it worried me that I stood in front of my closet half-naked and in a near panic, with rejected clothing strewn over my bed.

I wanted to look *good*. Better-than-Fiona good. Problem was, I didn't know how to do that. Fiona and I had opposing figure types. I was long and lean. She was average height and voluptuous. She had sleek, auburn hair in a cute stylish cut. I had an unchanging mop of curls. I flopped onto my back and groaned. There was no way I could compete.

My phone chimed and I startled. I'd set the timer so I knew when the countdown to Nate's arrival started. He was coming in a half hour, and I was nowhere close to ready! I jumped up with new determination. It'd been two weeks since I'd seen Nate in the flesh and I was going to look good. No, not good. Great!

I settled on jeans, a shiny silver T-shirt, and a soft, thigh-length cardigan over top. I clipped my hair up, letting a few strategic strands fall along my neck. Lucinda said my high cheekbones were my best feature, so I dabbed a pinch of sparkle there. Mascara and lip gloss. A spritz of perfume. I added my cross necklace, a birthday present from my dad that had crossed the ages with me. It served as a reminder to Nate about why we were *Nate and Casey*.

Satisfied with my looks I headed downstairs to wait in the living room. Dad was watching TV. He glanced at me and smiled.

"You look nice. Nate's in town?"

"Thanks, and yes."

"Isn't he going to Spain with his basketball team?"

I felt my smile drop. "Yeah. They leave on Sunday."

"That's a great opportunity for him."

Yes. It. Is.

I found myself staring at the front door, willing the door-bell to ring. I imagined myself stepping outside on the front porch, away from my Dad's prying eyes, and laying a good one on Nate's lips. He'd tell me I looked beautiful and I'd tell him he smelled good. We'd both be so happy and excited to finally be together after two weeks apart. We'd both be desperate to get in as much time as possible together before he left again for Spain.

The "F" word would not be mentioned.

I pulled my phone out of my purse and frowned. 7:03. Nate was late. He was always on time. Usually, early. I made another trip into the kitchen, stared into the massive refrigerator and closed the door without taking anything out. Again. I was like a lion in a cage, trailing a path. My heart ached with anticipation. The ticking from the clock on the wall seemed to grow louder. Now he was nine minutes late. I wrung my hands. *Nate, where are you?*

My ringtone sounded, and I sprinted to my purse to retrieve my phone. Nate's face looked back at me. I loved that shot of him—dark hair all tousled, blue eyes narrowing coolly. It was a video call so I pressed accept.

"Hey?" I said.

"Hi, Casey."

"Where are you?"

"Yeah, about that."

Something in his voice and the way he ran his hand across the back of his neck made me head upstairs to my room. "Is something wrong?"

"Yes and no. My parents surprised me. They came to town with my brother."

"John's back?" Nate's older brother John served in Iraq with the Canadian Army. "That's great!"

"Yeah. I'm so stoked to see him. The thing is, my parents made reservations in Boston for the four of us for dinner."

My heart sank. I lowered myself onto the edge of my bed. "I see."

"I'm afraid I can't see you tonight."

"Okay. Tomorrow then."

Nate grimaced slightly. "I can't. John's flying out of Logan at noon and wants to spend the morning with me, and Coach called a last-minute practice. I'm not coming into Cambridge at all."

I couldn't discern all the emotions that assaulted me with prickly tendrils at once. Disappointment, frustration and anger at John for picking this weekend to visit, annoyance at his parents for not including me (though I know I'm not technically family, but I have been a big part of Nate's life for over a year), hurt that Nate wouldn't find some way to see me, even if it were only for a few minutes (clearly, I'd been watching too many romantic movies lately), and sadness. I just missed him.

The winning emotion, however, was anger.

"That's fine," I said sharply. My eyes fluttered rapidly as I forced back the tears. "I'm busy, too. I have to get ready for my trip to Hollywood."

Nate's face flattened. "What?"

"I told you about the trip my creative writing class is going on."

"Yeah, and you said you weren't going."

"Well, now I am."

His eyes flashed with contempt. "You do know they *fly* coast to coast?"

"Yes, I know and I'll SLEEP." I was starting to sound like a broken record.

"Sleep?"

"On the plane. I never trip while sleeping. You know that."

"But what if you wake up? Casey!"

I rushed to explain my plan to abscond with my mother's prescription.

He snapped, "That's irresponsible."

"Maybe it's my turn to be irresponsible," I snapped back. I'd always been the good daughter, the good student, the good girlfriend. I was even the good time traveler. When did I get to sow *my* wild oats?

Nate ignored my comment. "It's dangerous."

"It's just a class trip. I won't get into trouble there."

"You get into trouble everywhere." Pain and anger cracked his voice. "Why not come with me to Spain? If you're going to live dangerously and irresponsibly anyway."

I wanted to go to Spain with him. Desperately. I sighed. "The flight there is twice as long." I could imagine knocking myself out for six hours, but twelve hours of travel with a stop meant two planes and double the risk. Besides that, only athletes, cheerleaders and coaches were allowed on the trip. I'd have to tag along as a solo, rather than part of the school group, which would present a whole slew of new problems.

Nate narrowed his eyes. "Don't do this just because you're mad at me."

"I'm doing it for me." I kept my voice light. "I'd decided to go to Hollywood before I knew you weren't coming tonight."

It was true. Mostly. I wasn't *that girl* who didn't have a life if she didn't have a boyfriend around. I was going to be *fine*. I was going to *have fun* in Hollywood. I would *live my own life*. Nate could *catch up to me* when he got back.

FOUR

I MOANED as a tap on my bedroom door was followed by Lucinda's sing-song voice. "Hey, sleepyhead, I've got coffee."

I cracked an eye to see a chipper Lucinda—wearing a fresh face, a long shimmering ponytail, cute jeans, blouse and spring jacket—standing over my bed with a to-go cup extended. I shifted into a sitting position as I accepted her offering.

She shifted onto my bed, settled on top of my silky quilt sitting beside me, and continued chattering. "I thought we could share date stories!"

Right. Her first date with Sam Capone. "How was Sam?" I murmured.

"Great! And Nate?"

"He didn't come."

"What?" Lucinda turned and took a good look at me. I knew my eyes were puffy because they felt like bowling bags. "Were you crying?"

"Some," I admitted. There was, in fact, quite a lot of tears and not so much sleeping during the night.

"Oh, Casey! What happened?"

I explained the "surprise" visit of Nate's brother and the coach's last minute call for practice.

Lucinda clucked. "That sucks big onions."

"I know."

"Well, it's not like he's going off to war. You will see him again soon."

"I know that. It's just, I'm used to seeing him all the time. Before he left for college we saw each other every day, and then once he was in Boston, at least once a week and we video chatted everyday. But lately, it's like he's too busy for me."

Lucinda wrapped her free arm around my shoulders and pulled me tight. "It's just a busy season. I'm sure everything is fine. You just need to keep busy with your *own* things. Live your *own* life. The time will go by in a snap and you'll have so much news to share with each other, you'll be sick of Nate by the time he finally lets you go."

This was why I loved Lucinda.

"I hope you're right," I said with a half-smile.

"I am right. Now do you want to hear about my date, or what?"

"Of course I do."

Lucinda talked animatedly for a good hour, and I was happy for her. Sam treated her well and I was glad she had someone now, too.

"Look, we took a selfie." She held her phone up for me to see. "Isn't he cute?"

Sam Capone had dark hair buzzed close to his head and

blue eyes, reminding me a bit like that guy from *Prison Break*. Lucinda leaned in close to him. Her eyes sparkled.

"You guys make a gorgeous couple," I said.

"Bonitos juntos!" she said in Portuguese. "Beautiful together."

When she left, I showered and made myself presentable, expecting a video call from Nate to come in at some point. He wouldn't leave the country without checking in with me once more, would he?

I ate a bowl of musli while watching sports TV with Tim and Dad, then headed to Mom's office to finish the filing she hired me to do. I was grateful Mom's business was doing well enough that she needed help. Otherwise, I wouldn't have had the money I needed to pay the deposit on Friday and now, with the awkward way things were with Nate, I was really glad for the distraction.

The special ring tone I had for Nate finally chimed after dinner. I rushed to my room for privacy before accepting the call.

"Hey?" he said tentatively.

I smiled softly. "Hey."

"Look, Casey, I'm sorry about last night. I don't want to leave with us on bad terms."

Awww. I knew he cared.

"I'm sorry, too. I know you didn't plan things to go the way they have. And really it's fine. I want you to have a good time."

He grinned that sideways grin that always made my heart flutter. "That means a lot to hear you say it."

"It's true. Besides, I'll be busy having a good time, too."

His smile dropped at that. "You're still going to Hollywood?"

"Yes," I said adding quickly, "You don't have to worry. I'll be back long before you will. You won't miss me at all."

"That's where you're wrong. I miss you already."

See? He did love me!

"I miss you too! But we can still video chat." Even though my trip west was adding an additional three hours to our time difference and we both had busy schedules. We'd just have to find a way to make it work.

"Yeah, I know." Nate sighed. "I gotta run. Early morning tomorrow."

"Okay. Have a safe trip. And watch out for clingy cheer-leaders." That last part just slipped out. I bit my lip expecting a rebuke, but Nate just rolled his eyes.

"I'll text when I get there," he said.

I wanted to kiss the screen, but that was gross, so I blew him a kiss instead. I kept the smile on my face until we disconnected, then slunk back on my fluffy pillow. I felt flat and hollow inside, but Lucinda's words resonated. "Do your *own* thing." I sat up, opened a clean document on my laptop and started a list of everything I had to do to get ready for my trip to Hollywood.

FIVE

I WAS DOING fine at school on Monday until Floozy sent me another instagram message. She was with her gaggle of cheerleaders in front of the Basilica Sagrada Familia. I recognized the tall narrow gothic towers from my research on Barcelona when I learned Nate was going there.

Wish you were here!

I stomped my foot. *Ohhh!* Even if I weren't aware of her penchant for sarcasm, I couldn't miss the smirk on her full-lipped face.

I was in a full-blown fury as I stumbled into creative writing.

"Hey, Donovan!"

My head swung to the low voice that called from one row over and one desk behind me.

Austin King?

He cocked his blond head and pierced me with his pale green eyes. "So you're coming to Hollywood?"

I blinked. Austin King was talking to me? Why?

Austin was a good-looking, popular guy who'd gone through a string of girlfriends since freshman year. I spent my first two years of high school as a social nobody and then when Nate came into my life, I rose to overnight celebrity status. Except for having Nate, I kind of preferred being invisible, it was *safer* with my condition, plus, I wasn't accustomed to the attention. I fell off the social radar again when Nate left for college. Every guy knew I was taken, so, unless there was a class project or other school-related reason to socialize, it just didn't happen.

"Yeah," I said, smoothing the look of confusion on my face.

"Your boyfriend's letting you go? I thought you were on a pretty tight leash."

What? That was what people thought? That I was controlled by my boyfriend?

"Nate's not *letting* me go," I said indignantly. "I didn't have to ask his permission."

"You're telling me he's okay with you coming on this trip? Unchaperoned?"

We weren't going to be unchaperoned. "Mr. Ryerson is coming."

"I don't mean by Ryerson, Donovan. I mean by Mackenzie."

Exasperated, I shook my head and turned my back to Austin King. Who did he think he was! I certainly didn't answer to him.

"Struck a nerve, huh?" he said.

Just ignore him.

I could ignore Austin King but I couldn't ignore the hot

feelings of anger he'd stirred up in me. I just couldn't tell if my anger was with Austin or with Nate.

Mr. Ryerson and his mustache called the class to order. "The list is now closed. For those of you who still need to deliver final payment..." His gaze landed on me. "Make sure you do so by the end of the day. I've confirmed those who have paid and tentatively booked flights for those who have not. We leave Thursday morning from Logan. Meet in the front parking lot at 7:00 am sharp to catch the bus to the airport." He handed out sheets of paper with the details printed on them. I plucked the check Mom had written for the remainder of the fee from my bag and handed it to Mr. Ryerson.

I carefully avoided looking at Austin as I walked back to my desk.

We spent the rest of the class working on our scripts. When the bell rang, I was surprised to find that Austin King followed me out of the room and kept pace with me down the hall.

I glanced at him sideways, feeling perplexed by his sudden interest. "What are you doing?" I finally asked.

"Walking. I think." He stared at the sneakers that peeked out of his hip-hugging jeans. "Yup. Walking."

"But why are you walking beside me?"

"Uh, do you have a no-go zone circling you? Last I heard, this was a free country and this particular hall is available to all registered students."

This guy was such a smart aleck!

He shoulder-bumped me playfully. "So what's your boyfriend doing while you're gallivanting across the country?"

I stopped short. Austin was the same height as me, maybe a smidgeon taller. I looked him straight in the eye. "Why do you care?"

He shrugged. "Just curious. I mean, I think I read somewhere that the Terriers were going to Spain."

"So?"

"You've been with Nate for a long time."

Again I said, "So?" Except maybe with a bit more feeling.

"First boyfriend?"

I started walking again. "What's with the first degree?"

He grinned. "I just think it's a shame that a pretty girl like you has never shopped around."

"What?" I stuttered to a stop again and stared at him. "Why would I do that?"

"Donovan, please don't tell me that you've only ever kissed one guy?"

I folded my arms and cocked my head. "Are you suggesting I kiss you?"

He smirked. "I'm a worthy candidate if you're looking."

Austin King was attractive, but super-duper arrogant. I picked up my pace. "No thanks."

I could hear him chuckling behind me. "Let me know if you change your mind."

I stopped at my locker, the last one of the row where the hallway intersected in a T-formation, to exchange my books for my last class. Austin King's unexpected conversation not only had my head spinning, but also had me running late for algebra. The halls were emptying out as other stragglers rushed to class. Just as I was about to slam my locker door shut, I heard male voices around the corner, and I froze.

"If he can't afford to pay, he can't afford to play."

"What do you want me to do, break his thumbs?"

A low chuckle. "A sprain will do for now."

I hid behind my locker door and watched as Sam Capone strode confidently down the hall, his back to me. I locked up my locker as quietly as possible and ran to class. I itched to get to Lucinda after the last bell to warn her about Sam, to tell her what I'd heard, and I could hardly concentrate on the assignment. I sighed. Just meant more homework for later. The class finally ended and I raced to meet Lucinda at her car, but I was too late. She was leaning against her bumper, holding hands with Sam Capone.

I relaxed my gait and forced a smile as I approached.

"Oh, Casey!" Lucinda said when she spotted me. She dragged Sam by the hand until we were standing in a close huddle. "I don't think you've officially met. This is Sam. Sam, this is Casey."

To my horror, Sam extended his hand to shake mine. I never, ever purposely touched anyone skin to skin for fear of bringing them back to the nineteenth century with me. My eyes widened and I stared hard at Lucinda. *Help me!*

Lucinda snatched Sam's extended hand and held it in her own. "Casey has, a condition, of the skin..."

Oh, God, she made it sound like I had a disease!

Sam's smile faltered, but he quickly recovered. "Nice to meet you."

I felt my face flush with embarrassment, and then I remembered the little convo I'd overheard and straightened my shoulders with indignation. *I know about you, buddy.* "Yeah, same," I said.

I waited in the passenger seat as Lucinda and Sam took much too long to say good-bye.

"Are you guys official now?" I asked when she slipped into the driver's seat.

Her face flared a warm crimson. "Yup." As we headed home, I tried to work it out in my head how I was going to tell her about what I heard.

"You really like him?" I asked.

"Yeah, I do. Why? You sound concerned."

"No, I'm not." Yes, I was. "He seems nice. Except..."

She cut me a look and I pointed to the windshield. "Eyes on the road."

She looked ahead and said, "Except?"

I hated to say anything, but the truth was, I'd heard rumors. I didn't want to say anything to Lucinda on Saturday morning because she was so excited and, let's face it, I was too exhausted. Plus they were rumors, but now I'd heard evidence myself.

"I've heard that Sam Capone is involved in an online gambling ring."

Lucinda responded sharply, "Not true."

"But.."

"It's *not* true. I've heard those rumors too, you know, and I straight up asked him. He admitted to playing the odd game of poker with his friends but nothing illegal."

"It's just that I heard..."

"Casey, they're *rumors*."

She was really defensive, but I'd known her long enough to know that when she made up her mind about something, no one could change it. And besides, I only overheard a couple sentences and maybe I was taking everything out of

context. They could've been talking about a school assignment or football for all I knew.

"You're still going to Hollywood?" she asked. She knew
today was the last day to pay up or bow out.

"Uh, huh," I answered. She wasn't the only one who
could be stubborn. She gave me the evil eye once she put her
car into park in my driveway. "I hope you know what you're
doing."

"About?"

"Flying." She squeezed my shoulder. It was a common
form of physical endearment because she didn't want to take
the chance of tripping back in time with me either. "I'm
worried. I'd hate for something to happen."

I offered a soft smile. "I'll be fine. Besides, I really need
this."

She nodded with understanding. "I know you do."

I spent an hour after school watching HGTV with my
mom. We both loved the makeover shows. Something about
taking a wreck and making it beautiful—it was an ugly duck-
ling story for homes.

My phone pinged, notifying me of a text, and I grabbed
it. Finally, a message from Nate.

But it wasn't Nate.

The message was from Austin King! No words, just an
image of a puckered set of kissing lips. Gah!

SIX

I was finishing up my algebra homework when I *finally* got a text from Nate.

Nate: Got here okay. Jetlagging though. Coach says to tough it out and play ball! Miss you.

Casey: Miss you too!

Nate: Bad news. I forgot to change my phone plan! Means it's going to cost a zillion dollars to call and text. Sorry!! Must to keep it to a minimum.

What? He forgot to change his phone plan? How could he do that?

Casey: Can you at least receive texts?????

I hoped he could read my panic and frustration in those question marks.

Nate: I don't know. Will have to limit use. But let me know when you get to Hollywood!

Ugh! This was awful. I'd imagined us texting and calling throughout our time apart. If I couldn't visit Spain, I at least wanted to hear about it and see pictures. I had planned to give Nate a play by play about my time in California. Now it was going to be a long, agonizing blackout.

I let out a long groan. At least I had Hollywood. It would be a distraction, and if I ever needed one, it was now. I forced myself to get off my bed, pulled my suitcase out of my closet and started packing.

I'VE ALWAYS BEEN a good kid. I guess time traveling from a young age made me responsible and resilient. I had to learn survival skills during my stints to the nineteenth century, always on alert and anticipating the unexpected. I had to be on my toes, one step ahead of the game. Because of this, I tried to keep my life in the twenty-first century as tame and uneventful as possible. I didn't feel the need to fight with my parents or rebel. With my world in the past being so uncertain and often dangerous, I longed for things to be as predictable and stable as possible on this side.

I tried not to lie to my parents. They didn't know about my other life in the past, so in a way that was lying by omission, and a big enough lie to convince me I had to balance things out by not lying otherwise. And sometimes, like when my stupid brother did stupid things, I was forced to lie to cover for him, but generally, I was a fan of telling the truth.

This was why, as I was packing my summer clothes for California, I found myself knocking on my mom's office door.

"Hey sweetie," she said as I entered. Her skin had paled to a winter white, but she'd gain some weight back and looked much healthier now than she had last summer.

"Mom? I need a favor."

She turned from her computer and lowered her glasses. "What is it?"

"I'm nervous about flying." The truth. Just not for the reasons she assumed.

Her expression softened. "Your chances of crashing in a car going into Boston are much greater than those of an airplane crashing in the USA."

"I know that, but I'm still nervous."

"Do you want to cancel?"

"No, I don't. I need to do this. Face my fears, and all that. Plus, I really think I want to be a writer, so this is too great of an experience to pass up."

She folded her hands on her lap and gave me her undivided attention. "What do you want to do, then?"

"Remember when Tim went missing?" I hated to bring it up. It was such a horrible time for her, and I cringed inwardly when her expression drooped. "And the doctor gave you a prescription so you could sleep?"

She frowned. "You want my sleeping pills?"

"Just for the flight. If I sleep, I won't spend the whole six hours white-knuckling."

"I don't think there are many left, only three or four, and I'm pretty sure I shouldn't share my prescription with you."

"They just make you sleepy right? And it's not like I'll get addicted if there's only a few left."

"I'll tell you what. I'll give them to you, but only if you promise you won't take them unless you absolutely need them. You might find that once you're up in the air, you actually enjoy it."

"Deal," I said, and it wasn't a lie. I absolutely did need them.

Mom retrieved the little blue container of pills, hesi-tating before dropping it into my hand. "For the record," she said, "I'm uncomfortable with this."

"I know, Mom. It's just a one-time deal, I promise."

I packed four pairs of shorts, three skirts and a dress along with an extra pair of jeans, a half-dozen shirts and sweaters, and underwear for the weekend, plus my hair and makeup products—and with hair like mine, wildly curly, there were a lot of hair products. I could barely get my suit-case closed. I wrestled with the zipper, using all of my body weight to hold the top down until it reached the end. There. I stood back and studied my bulging purple animal-striped suitcase. It looked like it ate a baby elephant.

I was ready for Hollywood. Only two more days to get through and *my* adventure would begin.

There was a light tap on the door, and before I could say, "come in," Tim was inside and sitting at my desk. Since the summer fiasco, he no longer wore guyliner or excessive amounts of cheap cologne in an effort to mask a temporary smoking habit. He did, however, walk with a limp. That unfortunately wasn't going away.

"Can I help you?" I asked, knowing that Tim wasn't here to ask for advice but to offer it.

"Okay, say you do manage to sleep for the whole flight and avoid a deathly tumble to the earth somewhere over Nebraska, what about when you get there? What happens if you visit California in 1863? You don't know anyone there. You don't have supplies hidden away."

"True," I said. "I don't know anyone and I don't have supplies, but California in 1863 is a lot safer place to be than Cambridge during that time."

The civil war was raging in the eastern states by the mid-1800s and navigating through those troubling times had gotten increasingly difficult. I missed the Watsons who had become like family to me, and their farm was a home away from home, but they had their hands full with the war, and it was best for all of us if I didn't go back there.

"I guess you got a point," Tim said. He knew better than anyone how dangerous it could be. He leaned forward and settled his pointy elbows on his knees. "I'm worried about you, Casey."

Awww. I flashed Tim a sisterly smile. "You know, I haven't tripped back since last summer, almost eight months. Maybe I've grown out of it. That's what Samuel said happened to him."

Tim's eyes widened with hope. "You think so?"

"Yes, I do. I've been plenty stressed these last few weeks," I said. Thanks to Fiona Frias the Floozy. "And I never tripped." I pointed to my eyes. "See, no dark rings. And I haven't spent the whole day in bed for ages."

Tim knew that these were the tell-tale signs of a return trip from the past: raccoon eyes and intense fatigue.

"I hope you're right," Tim said.

"I am right," I returned with newfound confidence. "This class trip to Hollywood is going to be smooth sailing. So don't worry about me. I'll be fine."

Dad drove me to the school early Thursday morning where I met up with my creative writing class. He got out of his Passat to shake Mr. Ryerson's hand and then gave me a hug good-bye.

"Thanks for letting me go," I said into his thick shoulder.

He rubbed my head. "You're welcome. Have fun, kiddo."

We loaded all our bags and gear on the bus. I sat beside an African American girl named Artimisha who had long tight curls kept off her face with a purple headband and wore round, clear plastic-framed glasses. The group was evenly split with eight boys and eight girls, which made it nice for sharing rooms. I knew everyone, some better than others, but none of them really well.

Turned out there was a lot to flying beyond finding your seat. You had to stand in a long line to check in, then you had to stand in another line to go through security, where basically everything you weren't wearing had to go through a scanning device and then you had to walk through a personal scanner and hope the beeper didn't go off. I made it through no problem but the bells sounded for Austin King. He smirked at me when he caught me watching. He'd forgotten to empty the change from his pockets.

Then there was another wait at the gate before we were called to board the plane. Our tickets and ID were checked once again before we headed down a long walkway and onto the aircraft.

That was the first moment my heart started to race. I downed two pills with water I'd purchased after we'd made it through security. I couldn't take any chances. I found my seat, by the window thankfully, so I could lean against it to sleep, put my purse under the seat in front of me and fastened my seatbelt.

Austin King stopped in the aisle and reached up to put his carry-on in one of the overhead bins, exposing a swath of tummy flesh as he did so. I had to admit that he had nice, toned abs. I couldn't help that I saw them, and it was true. I looked out the window and watched as the baggage handlers loaded the suitcases into the lower section of the plane.

I felt movement as the seat next to me was taken, and gasped when I saw who it was.

"Austin?"

"You called?"

"You're not sitting here."

"I'm not?"

"Let me see your boarding pass."

He grinned and pulled a crumpled piece of paper from his pocket. 18B. I double-checked mine. 18C. Of all the bad luck.

"What's the matter? Do I smell?"

I gawked at him. "No." He actually smelled pretty good, a fresh arctic scent. Which was worse.

He folded his arms. "Sorry to disappoint you, but here I am."

I yawned. "I'm not... whatever."

"Did you get my message?"

"What? You mean the lips?"

He laughed. "So you did get it." Then he puckered. "I'm ready when you are."

I punched him in the arm, which seemed to please him more than I would've liked.

I double-checked my seatbelt and thoroughly reviewed the In-Case-of-Emergency card, which was all drawings and no words.

"See this," Austin said. "If there's an unlikely loss of cabin pressure—" He changed his voice to sound happy and automated. "I, as the adult, will put my mask on first and then help you, the child."

I shot him a dirty look and decided to pretend he was a complete stranger who spoke a language I couldn't understand. I searched for the emergency exits and wondered briefly how I'd manage to find my way to one and actually hop out as breezily as the cartoon lady if I were in a drug-induced stupor. I caught Artimisha's eye two seats in front of me. She was checking out where everyone was sitting and she frowned when her gaze landed on me. Maybe because she had to sit next to Mr. Ryerson. I didn't think anything would be worse than sitting next to Austin King, but that would be worse.

The airplane moved, and a little yelp escaped my lips. I gripped the armrests and took a deep breath. Austin broke out in a hearty chuckle. "We're just taxying the runway, Donovan. Not much can go wrong yet."

"Leave me alone."

"Sorry, no can do. In fact..." He nudged my arm off the single arm rest between us. "That's mine, too."

"Fine." I pulled my arm in around my chest. I decided to keep my eyes focused out the window. The flight attendants did the safety demonstration and I double-checked my seat belt and counted the rows to the nearest exit. I leaned forward to check for the life jacket that was apparently tucked under my seat.

"What are you doing?" Austin asked.

"Checking for my life jacket."

Amusement flashed across his face. "We're flying over continental USA."

"Well... we might... there's the Mississippi. Or... why do they have life jackets then?"

"In case we get hijacked and are forced to fly over the Atlantic to Africa."

"What? Does that happen?"

Austin almost looked remorseful. "I'm just teasing you, Donovan. It's just normal aviation regulations."

I closed my eyes and prayed Mom's pills would kick in soon. Thankfully, I was starting to get really drowsy and I recalled what Tim had said about having a strong person to help me out. Austin was a strong person. He'd do. My eyes drifted closed. I meant to lean in against the window, but I suspected the opposite happened. I felt my cheek press against Austin's large bicep. It was the last thing I remembered before landing in LA.

SEVEN

THE NEXT THING I KNEW, someone with minty breath was shaking my arm and speaking into my face. "Donovan! Wake up!"

My eyes fluttered open, and I squinted confusedly at Austin's face. What was he doing in my room? Then my mind finally clicked in and registered where I was. Row 18 seat C.

I mumbled in response. "We're here?"

Austin nodded. "California dreaming."

"We're here!" Yay! I'd made it without spiraling to my death over Nebraska!

"You're pretty excited for someone who slept through the whole thing," he said with a glint in his eye. "Did anyone ever tell you that you snore?"

What? I looked at him aghast, then covered my mouth, which was *not* so minty. Then my gaze landed on a damp spot on Austin's shoulder, a darker blue splotch on his light blue T-shirt.

Oh, God. I'd drooled on Austin King's shoulder! I wanted to die! Why hadn't I hurled to my death in Nebraska??

I dug through my purse in search of a mint or a piece of gum and hurriedly popped a stray cherry lifesaver in my mouth. Then I busied myself by looking out the window as the aircraft taxied to the terminal. The sun shone brightly in the sky, too bright for early evening, I thought, but then I remembered the time change. We gained three hours, so it was only late-afternoon here. I checked my phone and noted how it had automatically adjusted the time to Pacific Standard.

The plane stopped, and everyone stood and gathered their belongings, but the flight attendants took their time to open the doors, so we all just stood there, some of us more disheveled than others, and tried not to get caught staring.

Austin was the exception. He made no effort to keep me from catching him from staring. Plus he was blocking my way to the aisle, and because of my height, I couldn't stand straight under the console above, so I shrunk back into my seat. Just as well. I still felt kind of woozy.

"What did you take anyway?" Austin said.

"What?"

"To make you sleep. Sure knocked you out. Why'd you do it? You afraid of flying?"

"No."

His lip pulled out like he'd caught me in a lie. It wasn't a lie. I wasn't afraid of flying. I was afraid of, you know, Nebraska.

I used the time to text my parents and Tim and Lucinda, to let them know I'd arrived safely. Lucinda sent me an animated emoticon showing intense relief. My heart squeezed as I thought of Nate. I shot him a two-word text. *Made it.* I hoped it didn't cost him too much to receive it.

I just couldn't believe he'd forgotten to change his phone plan! I had to give him the benefit of the doubt. He didn't do it on purpose so he'd have an excuse not to contact me. He was a really busy guy. He just forgot.

I felt myself growing angry about it anyway.

Finally, the bodies started to move and I dragged my carry-on awkwardly through the narrow aisles, the wheels of my small suitcase catching on one of every three seats.

Mr. Ryerson led the way to the baggage claim area and our group corralled around him.

"There's a bus waiting for us outside to take us to the hostel," Mr. Ryerson said. "We'll spend the night there, get our bearings, and in the morning join Ms. Bianco's creative writing class in the auditorium of Hollywood High."

Our bags inched their way out of a chute and onto a conveyor belt like a suitcase assembly line. I spotted mine with the purple animal stripes and squeezed through the crowd to pluck it off.

The first thing I noticed as we exited the glass doors on the ground floor of LAX was the warm dry air. I breathed it in—a mix of flowers and exhaust. This was great! I tugged my winter jacket off, the lightest one I owned, and tucked it under my arm.

All around us, up and down the shuttle bus lane, were tall palm trees. More than one convertible zoomed by and onto the exit that led into LA. I felt like I'd flown to a different country, not just a different state.

I craned my neck, looking out the bus window, taking it

all in. For someone who'd travel far into the past, I'd never actually traveled anywhere in my own timeline. My parents were busy with their jobs, and there was school, plus the whole marital breakup that had lasted for over a year put a wrench in family vacation planning.

I sat beside Artimisha on the bus, grateful that Austin King hadn't snagged the seat.

I glanced around, curious as to where Austin had landed. Which other hapless girl had to put up with his egotistical passes? He sat next to Spike, an Asian guy with cool hipster glasses. Austin caught me looking at him and winked.

Winked! I was appalled. I quickly averted my eyes.

"Have you been to California before, Artimisha?" I asked.

"Call me Misha, and yes," she said, pushing up her glasses. "We lived in California when I was a kid. My parents were struggling artists, once upon a time, before they moved to the east coast."

"Oh," I responded politely.

"I was three when my dad got a "real" job in Boston, so I don't remember California much. My grandparents live in Ohio, so that's where we go on vacation."

"Are you glad to be back here?"

Her eyes rolled back dreamily. "Yes. I'm going to UCLA in the fall. I've already been accepted."

"That's cool." I felt a weird and unwelcome sense of jealousy. I'd already been accepted in the BFA program at Boston University. It was what I wanted. To be with Nate and to study writing.

It was what I wanted.

We drove along a busy freeway, not as fast as you would

think due to major gridlock, and eventually headed into Hollywood.

"There's the sign!" someone shouted.

It was visible from the other side of the bus and I had to crane my head down and over to see it through an opposite window.

The big white letters, H-O-L-L-Y-W-O-O-D, sat crookedly propped up on the side of Mount Lee. It originally read Hollywoodland, I did a bit of research, and was only supposed to be a temporary sign to help promote a new real-estate development. Apparently, the development went under, but the sign was such a big draw, the community leaders decided to leave it. The "land" portion was removed because they wanted the sign to represent the whole area, not just the development property.

"So cool," Misha whispered. I agreed.

The bus turned down iconic roads like Sunset Boulevard and through the intersection of Hollywood and Vine. Palm trees lined every street. People walked around in light and loose clothing like it was the middle of summer. Graffiti tagged many of the businesses and kiosks. There were street musicians and costumed entertainers mixed with a multi-cultural crowd. So different than the serious, darkly clothed, grown-up vibe of Cambridge!

The bus pulled to the curb in front of our hostel, which was close to the center of Hollywood, and we tumbled out with new-world excitement. I practically floated away with glee—I was here! I'd traveled to the West Coast and lived to tell about it! I was ecstatic!

"Reign it in, Donovan." Austin King's eyes twinkled as

he grinned at me. "Your joyful enthusiasm is making the rest of us look like ungrateful snobs."

I felt my excitement seep out of me. "Am I embarrassing you?" I asked.

"Hardly. I find you incredibly amusing."

Any remnant of a smile left on my face dropped off at his comment. "So happy to entertain you."

"Now you're talking!"

"I was being sarcastic!"

"I know. The amusement never ends!"

I huffed and stormed away, and found a spot behind Mr. Ryerson. He was telling us the schedule for the rest of the evening, something about settling into our rooms, going to a nearby food court for supper and having an early night—but I could hardly concentrate. My mind furiously rewound the pseudo-conversation I'd just had with Austin King. Why did he rile me up so badly? Why couldn't I just ignore him?

I checked my phone and found messages there from Mom and Luce. Nothing from Nate. He'd been gone for two days and three nights and besides those first texts, I hadn't heard anything. We'd never gone this long before without some kind of communication. It was like he'd gone to the moon instead of to Europe.

Mr. Ryerson checked us in and handed out the room numbers. I was pleased I was rooming with Misha. She was quiet and level-headed and promised a drama-free experience. And I could re-assure her if need be that I was most definitely not interested in Austin King.

We ate supper at the food court, then our group walked around Hollywood at twilight, and because of the time change, we were ready to hit the hay at a decent hour.

I glanced in Austin's direction as we approached the entrance of our hostel, and he blew me a kiss. I rolled my eyes, even though I could feel my cheeks flushing. I checked my phone again, as if a message from Nate would magically appear. If only Nate would put in as much effort to get my attention as Austin did. I'd be happy with even a fraction of that.

EIGHT

THE NEXT MORNING, after a complimentary breakfast and coffee, we walked to Hollywood High. I hadn't realized how central the school was or how close it was to our hostel. I wore a denim skirt with a lacy white blouse and strappy sandals. Misha and I had taken some time the night before to paint our toenails and mine were a happy fuchsia. The morning was warming up nicely and I was glad I'd pulled my long dark curls into a high ponytail.

Austin had whistled at me when I stepped into view in the breakfast room. I pretended not to hear him and sat with Misha.

Misha grimaced. "What was that all about?"

"I honestly don't know. It's like some kind of switch went off in his brain when I signed up for this trip. He's been a hound dog ever since."

"He must like you," she said wistfully. "Maybe he was waiting for an opportunity to get you away from Nate."

I frowned at that. "Not possible."

Misha looked at me with swoony eyes. "It must be so nice to be in love. And," she added, "Nate Mackenzie is really cute."

I smiled knowingly. "Yes, it is. And he is."

Misha sat up straight and blinked at me. "How'd you do it?"

"Do what?"

"Snag an older guy."

"I didn't *snag* him. We... worked on a project together and became friends."

Misha eyed me as she sipped her orange juice. "Don't you worry about him being away in college? All those mature and experienced girls. As they say, 'when the cat's away the mouse will play.' I would go nuts. College/high-school relationships never last."

I was stunned by her sudden verbal diarrhea. My face heated with alarm. My chest tightened and I felt the need to breathe into my napkin. *Oh my God.* She was right! College/high-school relationships never *do* last.

No, some must. Surely, some must.

I choked the words out. "Some must."

Misha swallowed a spoon of cereal before looking me in the eye and finally seeing my torment.

"Oh, I'm so sorry, Casey. I didn't mean to be so insensitive. You have to excuse me. I don't have a filter."

"It's okay. You have a point. But Nate and I are different. We're soul mates."

Misha hummed. "Of course."

My appetite had taken flight with Misha's proclamations, but I forced myself to eat anyway. Last thing I needed was to faint in public due to low blood sugar.

Mr. Ryerson stood and clapped his pale, vein-lined hands. "Listen up Cambridge. Time to finish here and get ready to leave."

WE APPROACHED Hollywood High from the north, passing stores that were just lifting their window cages and pulling wares to the sidewalk, and souvenir and ticket hawkers that sought out tourists like us. Mr. Ryerson told us all to decline politely and to keep up. We came to the corner of Highland and Hawthorn and were awed by the famous mural of movie and TV stars who had graduated from this school. A gigantic John Ritter, and others including Laurence Fishburne, Cher and Bruce Lee. It was just so exciting to be here. I shifted my shoulder bag that contained my laptop, phone and personal items, and followed my class inside.

The theater was dimly lit and we shuffled down the slope of the aisle claiming empty seats. Mr. Ryerson went to the bottom of the stairs in front of the stage and greeted a woman I assumed was Ms. Bianco. My eyes adjusted to the dim light and I found myself searching the faces of the students who were lucky enough to go to school here full time. They were dressed more casually than we were and their skin had a sun-kissed glow whereas our group looked ghostly pale from months of winter. Even mine, and I had a slight natural tan.

My eyes locked onto the eyes of a blond girl from their

group who studied me as well. I felt like I knew her, but how was that possible? Her eyes also flashed with recognition, and suddenly I remembered. It'd been a couple years since I'd noticed her in a Cambridge convenience store.

It was when I thought Nate was going to end our friendship after I'd accidentally taken him back to 1860. That would freak anyone out and I wouldn't have blamed him for saying adios and hightailing it as far away from me as possible. It had been a hot late-spring afternoon and I'd stopped at the corner store for something cold to drink. A girl with a long blond ponytail who was dressed like Sandy from Grease (before she totally changed who she was just to get the guy) had reached for a soda at the same time I did. I remembered she had worn a bracelet with her name. Adeline.

I stared at her profile from across the auditorium. Her face had matured, thinner with higher cheekbones, and her hair was cut shorter and bleached lighter.

I missed the name of the guest pro scriptwriter who was introduced, but he must've been well known in LA because a huge hoot went up from the Hollywood High kids.

The man was in his mid-thirties with a slightly receding hairline. He wore a tight, black graphic T-shirt and had tattoos running from elbow to wrist. "Thanks for having me," he said without smiling. "Let's get started. Today we're going to breakdown the classic time travel comedy, *Back to the Future.*"

I shot a look across the room to Adeline. Her neck craned to look back at me. Had she recognized me, too? Her lips pulled up into a knowing smile. I grinned back.

I refocused on the scriptwriter. " ...The inciting incident, also called the catalyst, is when Marty McFly meets up with Doc Brown in an empty mall parking lot to experiment with a souped-up DeLorean. When the car suddenly disappears leaving only a track of flames, Marty learns the doc was experimenting with time travel."

His Power Point flipped to the next plot point. "Can anyone tell me what plot event happens to catapult the story into the second act?"

AFTER THE LECTURE, there was time to mingle and Adeline and I both inched our way in the direction of the other.

"Are you Adeline?" I asked just to confirm.

She nodded. "Yeah. I'm sorry I don't remember your name."

"Casey."

Her lips, which were a bright cherry red, widened into a grin. "This is so cool! I honestly didn't think I'd ever see you again. You wouldn't believe how many times I'd kicked myself for not getting your contact info."

"Same! Do you still... "

Adeline nodded. "But not so often, anymore."

"Me too. I haven't tripped since summer."

"Trip. Right. I remember now that you called it that."

Mr. Ryerson clapped his hands again, gaining our attention. Our next stop was Grauman's Chinese Theater, which was in walking distance.

"Are you guys coming?" I asked Adeline.

"Nah. We've done all the tours. But we're having a BBQ together tonight, so we can meet up later."

"Great," I said. "We have a lot to catch up on!"

"I know!"

I contemplated this happy reunion as we walked north on Highland and west down Hollywood Boulevard. It felt so good to know there was another person on this planet, a person my age, who was like me. I wished I could tell Nate. I retrieved my phone—it was on vibrate for school—and stared at the screen. Still nothing from him. Spain was nine hours ahead of the west coast and he was probably sleeping.

I thought Austin might've moved on from his brief infatuation with me, but once we hit the Boulevard, he snuck up from behind and became my shadow.

"Pretty cool, hey?" he said. I agreed. The whole California vibe was cool. The hills were green, the sky was blue and most of the smog that had lingered in the morning had burned off.

We jostled down the crowded sidewalk, and I was glad I wore a light sweater to prevent unwanted skin-to-skin contact.

The Grauman's Chinese Theater was a bodacious architectural venture with long curvaceous lines, bright colors and tall dog statues that were imported from China when the theater was built. The building was enough to demand a person's attention, but my focus was on the famous cement imprints of the hands and feet of famous movie stars.

Misha pointed. "There's Mary Pickford! And Douglas Fairbanks."

We'd studied film history and had learned that Mary Pickford had been a super huge silent-film star. Her engagement and marriage to Douglas Fairbanks ranked as high in popularity around the world as when Prince Charles married Lady Diana. They were American royalty, the current Brad Pitt and Angelina Jolie of their time.

She'd become quite the businesswoman, too, and was originally part-owner of the Chinese Theatre.

I knelt down and pressed my hands in Mary Pickford's imprints and laughed. "I'm such a giant!" My fingertips extended far beyond the star's.

"She was a petite woman," Misha said. "That's how she got all those child roles."

We stood in line to get inside the theater and I felt a warm body press up against my back. I took a step forward, inwardly cursing the crowds, and crossed my arms against my chest, making sure I wasn't touching anyone. The body behind me shifted forward, too. I turned on my heel, prepared to politely ask whoever it was to step back, but I found myself staring into Austin King's green eyes.

Of course.

"A little space, please," I said.

"I think you should give me a chance," he said, shuffling up beside me.

"Chance for what?"

"To be your boyfriend."

"I already have a boyfriend."

"Yes, I know. But like I said before, you need to spread your wings. Dip your toes in other pools of water. You're too young to settle on the first guy who shows interest in you."

My shackles raised in offense. "I'm not settling, and who cares if he was the first person to notice me like that? Why didn't you notice me back then if you're so great?"

"I did notice you. All the guys did."

"Shut up."

"I'm serious."

I huffed. "You didn't notice me until ten minutes ago."

"That's not true. The guys noticed you. Maybe not the jocks, but the kind I hung with did. You weren't exactly approachable, you know."

I had to concede that.

He tilted his head, letting muddy blond locks fall into his eyes. "You intimidated me."

I shot him a look. "I don't think anyone intimidates you."

He laughed. "Maybe not now, but then, I was just a shy kid."

Austin pushed his hair off his face and held my gaze. "Look, Casey. You're beautiful and smart. Which is why I can't understand why you're not being more open minded. How do you know I'm not the right one for you if you don't give me a chance?"

"I can't. I love Nate. We're a couple. I'm sorry."

Austin shoved his fists into his jeans pockets and looked at me sheepishly through dark lashes. "You can't blame a guy for trying."

He was a good-looking guy. Suave and persuasive. "I'm certain you'll find another girl soon."

He chuckled. "I haven't exactly given up on you yet, Donovan." He flashed me a smile before jogging to the front of the line to join Spike and Thomas.

I pushed Austin's words from my mind while I dragged through my purse for my phone. *Please let there be a message from Nate.* I sighed at the empty screen, then thumbed a message.

Casey: I'm at Grauman's Chinese Theatre! Wish you

were here!! Can't wait to hear about Spain. Are you winning?

I wanted to go on, but I didn't think he'd appreciate my long windedness, especially if it was going to cost him a zillion dollars.

NINE

THE BBQ WAS HOSTED by the family of one of the students in Adeline's group, a small girl with long dark hair and a lot of facial piercings, who walked with a leg brace. She also sported the fancy starlet-type name of Bluebell. We were told that her father was a studio hot-shot, but I'd never heard his name before. They lived in an impressive home in Hollywood Hills that boasted a pool and a multi-million-dollar view of the Los Angeles area all the way to the ocean twenty-five miles away.

I spotted Adeline immediately. She wore an A-line skirt that ended well below the knee and had bright orange lipstick on her full lips. Her bleach-blond hair was parted on the side into a fat-curl bob. She stood on the other side of the pool. From a distance, she really did look like Marilyn Monroe.

She was in the middle of a friendly conversation with Bluebell and a nice-looking guy I hadn't seen in the scriptwriting class who looked like he'd rather be surfing.

Adeline looked my way and I waved to catch her attention. She smiled and motioned for me to join them.

"Hey, Casey. Have you met Bluebell? She's in our scriptwriting class."

"Not officially," I said. I waved my fingers and tucked my hand behind my back before Bluebell tried to shake hands.

Adeline threaded an arm through the guy's tanned elbow. "And this is my boyfriend, Marco."

I nodded. "Hi."

"Marco surprised me by showing up tonight," Adeline said. "He was supposed to leave for a family event today, but his trip was postponed until tomorrow."

"That's great," I said. "How long will you be gone?"

"Just a few days," Marco said. His gaze dropped to his feet before flickering to Adeline's, and it was obvious that they had a strong thing going by the way their eyes lit up when they looked at each other. His fingers ran down her arm until they were clasping hands. I swallowed down a lump of envy. I hadn't seen Nate for almost three weeks and hadn't heard from him in four days.

"I'm going to see how things are doing in the kitchen," Bluebell said. She limped away, carefully dodging patio furniture and students lounging about.

"Marco," Adeline said with a purr, "would you mind getting us something to drink?"

"Sure," he said. He pulled his hand free and gave us a friendly smile before heading for the drink station on the other side of the pool.

"He seems nice," I said.

"He is," Adeline agreed.

"Does he know?"

She surprised me by shaking her head. "I've tried to tell him, but he doesn't believe me."

"Really? But the way he holds your hand... you've never taken him back?"

"No. Not that I've been especially careful, as you can see." She shrugged a shoulder. "It just hasn't happened."

"How long have you been together?"

"A year and a half."

I was shocked by her answer. A year and a half with one guy and he still didn't know about this other part of her life?

"I've been with my boyfriend Nate for that long, but he knows all about it."

Adeline's eyes widened with surprise. "I'm not sure what Marco would do if it happened. He's already convinced I need therapy."

Marco returned with two sodas before we could go any deeper. Knowing Marco wasn't acquainted with our lifestyles, I refrained from asking more questions. I could tell by Adeline's look that she had more she wanted to say to me, too.

"Did I interrupt something?" Marco said at our silence.

"Just girl talk," Adeline said, and then she added, looking at me. "We'll catch up some more later, okay?"

I nodded and watched them walk away together.

Bluebell's parents were curiously absent. The whole affair was catered by their kitchen staff and overseen by Mr. Ryerson and Ms. Bianco. They introduced ice-breaker games to get us to interact with the Hollywood High students and then finally announced that the food was ready.

I took a seat at one of the many tables erected for the occasion and drank in the view. The horizon sparkled with lights as the day turned to twilight. I wondered what had happened to Misha and searched the party for her. She was looking my way as she stood in line for her food. I waved her over. She made some kind of hand signal I couldn't decipher. She knew where I was if she wanted to find me. I spotted Adeline and Marco standing near the pool. They were talking intensely to each other, both with deep frowns on their faces. Their easygoing style had turned into something much more intense.

Someone dragged a chair beside me, and I looked to see Austin taking a seat.

He was persistent if nothing else. I had to give him that.

I nibbled on Cobb salad and a BBQ chicken leg.

Austin had a mound of food on a paper plate, and it was quite an event to watch how fast he consumed it.

"Impressive," I said.

He pushed a pile of bones to the side. "Thanks. Years of practice."

I found my gaze cutting to his profile. Austin had a nice face, strong cheekbones and a chin covered with blond bristles that glinted in the rays of the setting sun.

"Why don't you have a girlfriend?" I asked. It seemed blunt, but he hadn't exactly been Mr. Subtle.

He faced me and parted his lips into a smile. "Just waiting for the right one to come available."

"Uh-huh." My eyes zeroed in on those lips. They were different from Nate's, but nice.

To my horror, Austin noticed. He smirked and pointed to his face. "See, you want to try these out, don't you?"

"No, I don't!"

"Sure you do. You've only kissed one guy." He smacked his lips. "Any time you wanna have a go, just let me know."

I scoffed in an effort to distract from the flush of embarrassment heating my cheeks. I covered my eyes and muttered. "Don't hold your breath."

His phone buzzed and he pulled it out of his back pocket.

"News from home," he said.

"Oh?" I reached into my bag for mine, grateful for the change in subject. "I didn't know we had wifi here."

Austin's lips pulled down into a frown.

"What is it?"

"I don't think you want to see."

Now I was curious. "What?" My phone was taking too long to link up.

"It's the Terrier's Facebook site."

I'd been following, but hadn't had a chance to check it since the morning. At that time, there had been no new updates.

"Are they losing?" I reached for his phone. "Let me see."

He pulled his arm back so the phone was just out of my reach. "No, they're winning. And celebrating."

I extended my arm again. "Please?"

He gazed hard at me with eyes that looked worried.

"Austin!"

"I don't think you want to see this."

"Why?" I reached for him again. This time he hesitantly placed his phone in my palm and I stared at it in disbelief. My heart squeezed like a heavy foot had stepped on it. Nate's foot.

It was a cheerleader after-game party shot. Fiona had

one arm wrapped around Nate's neck, an over-flowing beer mug in the other, and she was planting a big kiss on Nate's cheek. His eyes were closed, and the shot was kind of blurry, but you didn't have to be a brain surgeon to see that they were together.

My throat clogged up, and I couldn't suppress the tears that filled my eyes. Austin's arm slipped around me, and I found myself crying into his neck. He smelled good. Musky and manly.

Next thing I knew, his lips were on mine. And stupid, stupid me, I kissed him back.

TEN

I PLACED two hands on Austin's chest and pushed sharply, breaking free from his lips.

"What are you doing?!"

He cocked a brow. "I think the question is what are *we* doing?"

"Oh, God." I buried my face in my hands. I felt sick.

"It's not that big a deal, Casey. It's just a kiss."

It was a big deal. It was cheating! Here I was all worried and upset about the Floozy throwing herself at Nate and the first opportunity I had to kiss another guy, I moved my tongue! And I wasn't even drinking!

What was the matter with me???

I jumped to my feet and ran, not even caring that I was bumping into people. I felt dizzy and awash with light.

Oh, no! I was about to trip back in time just like Tim warned me, and it was all Austin King's fault! I accidentally ran into one of the girls, and she began to topple into the pool and reflexively grabbed at what was next to her, which happened to be me. Skin on skin!

I followed her into the water, swallowing a good amount of chlorine in the process.

My legs flailed as I tried desperately to touch the bottom. My fingers ran along the vinyl lining before I managed to get my footing. Then suddenly I was standing, dripping wet, on dry ground. The pool was gone. The students were gone. Bluebell's house was gone.

I heard panting behind me and turned to see Adeline Savoy. She was the girl I'd knocked into the pool.

"Casey?" Adeline said. "Was it you or me?"

"I think it was me."

Adeline's drenched clothing clung to her curvaceous form, her short blond hair a wet cap on her head. I glanced down at my equally soaked body, tall and slim. We both wrapped arms around our shivering bodies. The sun was about to set, taking its daytime warmth with it.

I took in our barren surroundings. Dirt roads doodled the hillside along with short wooden stakes marking new lots. In the distance I spotted a new house under construction, and on the hill beyond were the big letters spelling out Hollywoodland.

We were in the past, but not 1863.

"It' must've been you," I said. "The 1950s?"

Adeline shook her head. "Something's off." She studied the Hollywoodland sign with an expression of confusion, "That sign..."

A motor caught our attention and we turned to the direction of the sound. A car came sputtering into view. Not a thick, rounded-body automobile one expected to see in the fifties, but a black jalopy. Big narrow wheels, its body looking more like a carriage than a car. It zoomed by, kicking up dust, backfiring on its way past.

"Was that a Ford Model T?" I asked. "It looked brand new."

A second car much like it passed by in the other direction. I stared at Adeline. "*When* are we?"

She shook her head again, and a flash of unease crossed her face. "I have no idea, but this isn't my time."

I stated the obvious. "It's not mine either."

I rubbed my goose-pimply arms. "Maybe, against incredible odds, we both tripped at the same time. And the fact that we were touching while it happened caused a reset?"

Adeline scrunched her nose. "Met somewhere in the middle?"

We shared a worried look. "We need to find out what year this is," I said, "and find a place to spend the night."

Adeline nodded in agreement. "Let's go." We headed toward the dirt road and down the hill.

It was a decent trek to civilization, but at least my skirt and blouse were drying out somewhat. I removed my sweater and hung it over my arm to give it a better chance.

I knew what had triggered my trip, *the kiss*, but I wondered what had triggered Adeline's. I remembered the tense conversation I'd witnessed from across the pool. "Did you and Marco have a fight?"

Her bottom lip inflated. "You could say that."

I didn't know her well enough to probe further. It wasn't my business. It was just pure bad luck that we both happened to be tripping at the same time while touching each other. The chances of that ever happening were slim to none, so of course it would happen to me.

We reached the bottom of the hill and I stopped, realizing I had no clue where I was. "Lead the way," I said to Adeline. "You know this place."

Her brow furrowed between wide-set blue eyes. "I know it in the twenty-first century and in the 1950s," she said. "It looks a lot different now."

We made it to a main street, and I spotted a road sign that said Hollywood Boulevard. The street was filled with Model Ts or vehicles that looked very similar. The road rules of the day seemed to need regulation and crossing the road looked perilous. Dusk required headlights, which looked like big bug eyes, and the streets were infested. A street car, a blend between a bus and a rail car, motored down tracks in the middle of the lane and pedestrians crossed anywhere that suited them. Compared to modern times, the traffic flow was slow, but still, I wouldn't want to get hit by a jalopy.

"We should keep out of bright lights," I said. We weren't dressed right for this era, which was obvious by what the pedestrians wore. The girls had short hair, some with small hats or headbands, and some with feathers, and loose, layered dresses that ended at the knees. Most wore waist-length jackets with fur collars. "I'm guessing we've landed somewhere in the 1920s."

"Yup," Adeline said. "The question is what year."

I'd only ever been to the late nineteenth century and only ever in Massachusetts. I felt shaky and uncertain as I followed Adeline.

"We should go back to the school," she said. "It's the only place I can think of where we can get shelter for the night.

Maybe find some appropriate clothes." She led us through back alleys and down darker roads with confidence. She was only off her era by three decades and knew the street layout. I was really happy to have her along. This was so much more comforting than traveling back in time alone, especially in a new region and a new century.

"This is it," Adeline said. "Hollywood High in the 1920s."

I barely recognized the school. There were several buildings on the property, but they looked different from what I'd seen in the present. The main building sat facing Highland, rather than Sunset, and it was way cooler looking. Three stories with a smaller portico tucked into a larger one and each with its own set of Greek columns. I ran up the long cement steps and peered through the front door. Inside I could see a banner: Class of '29.

"It's 1929," I called out. I already knew we were in the roaring twenties, but the reality of it still left me feeling stunned.

"We need to find the drama department," Adeline said.

A house occupied the land where the future auditorium would one day be built. I followed her to the back of the building. She peeked into the windows. "Look for props and costumes."

I cupped my hands over the glass and squinted into the dark rooms where I could barely make out rows of desks or shelves of books. Then I found one that broke the mold. It lacked the desks and there was a stage along the back wall. "Here," I said. "This is it."

Adeline hurried to peer inside and then said, "We need to break in."

It was dark—time of day doesn't always line up—and I was glad for the moonlight. I scoured the ground for a tool and spotted a large jagged stone nestled in a tuft of grass along the foundation. I locked eyes with Adeline and she nodded her chin. "Go for it."

"Alarms?"

"Not in 1929."

I used my pitching arm and threw the rock, wincing as the glass cracked and shards dropped to the ground.

Adeline carefully picked pieces of glass away until the hole was large enough for her to poke her arm through. She flicked the lock, then slid the window open.

ELEVEN

SINCE I WAS TALLER and more lithe than Adeline, I offered to go first. I inched through the window, aware that I might be flashing my undies, but that was the least of my worries. My wild curls got caught on the bracket, and I yelped a little as I jumped in. I spotted a floor lamp in the corner and turned it on. Its weak bulb shed a warm, cozy light. Then I unlocked the door and let Adeline inside.

The room was twice as long as it was wide. Props of various types were piled on the shelves along one wall and clothing hung on racks next to it. I immediately went to the dresses and started flipping. Up to now, we'd had the advantage of darkness to cover our contemporary dress, but that would change come morning.

There were dozens of flapper dresses, a type of dress that had no waist or emphasis on the bustline, just straight lines like a fancy bag with a hole for the neck. I held one up against my body, guesstimating that it would fit, and pulled the flapper dress over my blouse and short skirt. It was a soft creamy satin with layers of fringe, like a lampshade, from the waist down. I swiveled my hips causing the fringe to shake and shimmer. "What do you think?" I asked.

Adeline smiled. "Looks good!"

She found a blue dress similar to mine but didn't put it on. "We need to get some sleep," she said. "We have to make sure we're out before the kids and teachers arrive in the morning."

Adeline curled up on a purple chaise lounge in the corner and closed her eyes. I fell onto a green one next to it. Traveling was exhausting. I shut my eyes, shifting a few times before I floated away into dreamland.

Adeline nudged me awake at the first light of dawn.

I stretched and worked out the kinks as the events of the previous evening washed over me. I'd hoped it'd all been a bad dream, especially the part where I'd cheated on Nate, but my unfamiliar surroundings and the sight of Adeline proved that it was all too real.

Adeline shimmied into the dress she'd chosen the evening before. Unlike me, she removed the fifties-styled clothes she was wearing before putting it on.

"What should I do with these?" she asked. "I don't think I should leave them around for someone to find."

"There's a trash can over there," I said, pointing. She discarded her twenty-first century vintage fifties clothing knowing she'd get them back when she returned. It was just one of the mysterious rules of time travel. When you returned to the present, you arrived at the exact moment you left, which meant you once again wore what you had on in that moment.

"At least you have short hair already," I said. I ran fingers through my long, dark locks. "What am I going to do with this?"

"We can make a faux bob," Adeline said. There was a makeup table with combs and brushes, and many hair pieces hanging from hooks on the wall. "I saw a Youtube video once on how to create a short hair look. That was before I had the courage to take the scissor plunge."

I sat on the chair in front of the mirror. Adeline split my hair into two layers and put the bottom layer into a long braid, which she then pinned up in an elongated bun at the nape of my neck. With the top layer, she did some fancy back-combing and pinned it up underneath, securing it to the braid. The end result was me looking like I had short hair.

"Nice job," I said, admiringly.

She plucked a yellow headband off the wall and added it. "There," she said. "That looks authentic."

Adeline's hair was short, but styled more for the fifties than the twenties. She plopped a black fitted hat on and plucked out a few blond strands, smoothing them down and tucking them in, just so. "Now for makeup," she said. "They wore a lot of it in the twenties."

Adeline applied makeup like it was second nature. Soon her eyes were dark and smoky, exaggerated with thick eyeliner and mascara. She applied blush in rosy round circles. I stared at her with wonder.

"How do you know what to do?"

She pointed to the wall. Several posters of what I assumed were famous actors were pinned up. Adeline looked just like the women in them.

"Do you want me to help you?" she asked.

I nodded, conceding that I was pretty clueless when it came to makeup. She went to work and by the time she was done, I barely knew my own face.

Adeline plucked a couple long necklaces from a drawer. "Here, take one of these."

I lifted a strand of green beads carefully over my hairdo and let them fall over my chest. Adeline donned several strands of pearls.

"This is kind of fun," she said.

"Yeah," I said, though I wasn't sure how long it would last. We needed to get going soon and who knew what we'd find when we did. Hopefully, there would be some food involved. If it came down to it, we could hunt small birds, but I'd need to fashion a slingshot for that. It was a last resort. Thinking of food triggered a stomach growl.

Adeline chuckled. "I'm hungry, too."

I dug through things I found lying on a bench by the door. Opening a brown bag, I pulled out an apple. "Someone left their lunch behind."

I took a bite and passed the apple to Adeline. She chomped on it and gave it back. "There's a sandwich," I said. I sniffed it. "Smells all right."

We both jumped at the sound of the doorknob clicking. Someone was unlocking the door! Adeline and I stared wide-eyed at each other, then our time travel survival instincts kicked in and we dashed to the clothing rack and crouched behind it.

Whistling filled the room, a tune I didn't recognize, and through a slender space between dresses, I saw a middle-aged man enter the drama room. He wore drooping trousers that narrowed to his ankles, a vest and jacket over a white shirt with a brown bow tie and a fedora on his head. He shucked off his jacket, hung it on a hook and placed his hat on the shelf above.

He turned and started walking straight toward us! I grabbed Adeline's hand in the off chance that one of us might conveniently trip and held my breath. I tried to think of a plausible excuse as to why two strange girls would be hiding behind the dress rack. Just as he was about to reach us, he made a sudden detour to his right and stopped in front of the vanity mirror. He ducked and examined his face, running a finger over his moustache, smoothing it out, and then did the same to each of his eyebrows. He combed his hair back and hummed with satisfaction, apparently liking what he saw.

I worried he'd return to the dresses, but then he suddenly caught sight of the broken window.

He growled, "What the heck?" He stepped over to examine the damage and shook his head. "Darn kids!" Then he hurried out the door.

I straightened and groaned at the kink in my back. "That was close."

Adeline agreed. "Let's get out of here."

We ducked out the door, making sure the drama teacher was out of sight, and hurried until we were off the property and safely on Hawthorne Avenue. I stopped to take it all in.

Hollywood 1929, here we come.

TWELVE

We spent a couple hours taking in the sights. I mean, that was one benefit of time traveling. Who got to do this kind of sightseeing?

The sidewalks were full of women dressed in layered, straight-seamed dresses, adorned with several strands of long pearls and beads and many with feathers in their caps. There were others dressed plainer, but they still blended in. Some of the older women wore long skirts, cinched at the waist that touched boot-like shoes, and white long-sleeved blouses, their hair in buns on the top of their heads—throwbacks from the previous decade. Men strolled in suits and leather shoes, tipping their hats as they passed by.

The streets rumbled with Model Ts and the like zigzagging around each other, dodging pedestrians and old street cars that groaned with the effort.

"My dad would love this!" Adeline said. "These old cars are in mint condition."

"They're not old yet, but they are cool," I said. "I bet they'd be fun to drive."

Adeline's eyes glinted mischievously. "Maybe we should go for a joyride."

I was shocked. "Steal a car?"

"Not steal. *Borrow*."

I stared at her in surprise. "Do you know how to drive?"

Adeline rolled her eyes. "No. That would be hazardous. I'm just joking around."

Hollywood was a comparatively small town in 1929 with more agricultural land and less sprawl. The hills were still in their natural state, unmarred with the extensive subdivisions found in my real time.

We happened across an orange grove, beautiful with its orange globes hanging against the dark green leaves of the trees.

"I've never seen an orange tree before," I said.

"I know, hey?" Adeline said. "I'd never seen one either before my dad and I moved here from Cambridge. She swallowed. "They remind me of how thirsty I am."

"My throat's parched, too." I held her gaze. "Shall we?"

She nodded and I followed her into the grove, stepping carefully through the long grass. We each plucked an orange, settled into the grass and began peeling.

In my own time, I never took things without paying, and I hated justifying it when I tripped, but the fact was, if I didn't take and borrow, I wouldn't survive. I made it a policy to only take what was absolutely necessary and to replace things when I could.

I slurped on the fruit, leaning forward over the grass as to not slush juice onto my dress. Adeline did the same and it made me smile. It felt great to have a partner in crime. Not a non-traveler I had to look out for and protect, but a person who *knew*. Someone skilled and adept in time-travel life. Even if I tripped home without her, I knew she'd manage on her own and get back eventually.

At least I thought I knew that.

I wiped my mouth with the back of my hand and tossed the peels. "What if we screwed it up?"

Adeline adjusted her black cap as she eyed me. "Screwed what up?"

"The loop. I mean, I used to loop to the 1860s and you to the 1950s. We'd loop back in time and then return to our present. This accidental trip is an anomaly. It's not part of our natural pattern."

"Yeah?"

"So what if we don't loop back? Or maybe we'll loop back to an entirely different time. My particular writing class might not be the one I return to." My imagination began to run away. I envisioned endless tripping from one year to another and never getting back home to my present. Never able to make things right with Nate. A ribbon of panic pulled against my ribs.

"Casey!" Adeline snapped her fingers. "Get a grip. We have to keep our heads."

"I know, I know, it's just, this is unfamiliar territory."

"How long do you usually stay when you trip?" Adeline asked.

"It varies. Sometimes just a few hours, sometimes three or four weeks."

"Same." She stood and brushed grass off the back of her

dress, the fringe on her layers shimmying back and forth as she did it. "Let's just assume we'll get back…"

Until we don't.

"We have to find a way to make money," I said, "if we're going to be here for any length of time. Or find a family to help us."

"Agreed."

"Hey!" A man's voice shouted through the grove. He wore overalls and had a deep tan. He pointed angrily at us.

"Busted," Adeline said. "Let's dash."

We ran away from the orchard worker as fast as we could and kept running until we hit the street. We didn't stop until we were certain no one was after us and then we bent over, panting to get our breath.

I caught Adeline's eye, and she broke out in a cackle. Her laughter was contagious and soon I couldn't stop myself from laughing out loud along with her. Not because it was funny, but because it wasn't, and we were in such a new and scary situation, and all that stress—just made us laugh the harder.

I wiped tears from my cheeks and worked to catch my breath. "I hope we're not going crazy."

"Me, too," Adeline said. "It's only the first day."

We eventually made it back to Hollywood Blvd, though neither of us knew exactly what we were looking for.

Adeline pointed to a building with a long brown awning that stretched over the sidewalk. "That's Brown Derby Restaurant. Lots of stars apparently hung out there."

Just then, a glamorous couple exited.

Adeline gasped. "That's Mary Pickford. And Douglas Fairbanks!"

We stared at the famous couple. We weren't the only ones gawking. All the pedestrians stopped where they were. Many shouted out the actors' names and waved enthusiastically. The Pickford/Fairbanks duo drove away in a convertible buggy car, waving calmly, like they were used to all the attention.

Once the spectacle was over, everyone continued at their normal busy pace, like a slow-mo button had been released.

There were so many cars on the road, it was hazardous for pedestrians to cross. Policemen stood on short boxes in some of the busier intersections, directing traffic. Everyone had to look out for the streetcars that rumbled down the middle of the road in both directions. There was honking and beeping and shouting by angry drivers: road rage in its infancy.

I pointed to a sidewalk sign ahead that read, "Movie Extras needed!"

"Maybe that's our answer," I said.

A woman, maybe in her mid-twenties, manned a small table. She had bobbed blond hair with expertly done finger waves and she puckered her red lips. She wore a green flapper dress with several long strands of pearls around her neck.

Adeline and I took a moment to make adjustments to our bedraggled appearance.

I spun around. "Do I look okay?"

She tightened a couple pins on the back of my head. "There. You look great. How about me? Is my makeup still okay?"

I studied her face. "Yup. You look good."

"Okay," she said with a deep breath. "Let's roll."

We approached the girl and smiled. "Hello," I said.

"Ya lookin' for movie work?" The woman spoke each word with a sharp, staccato beat. Adeline surprised me by replying with the same cadence.

"How do we sign up?"

"Ya need to be eighteen years old and available for this afternoon. It's for three hours work and the pay is a dollar thirty."

"Per hour?" I asked.

She flashed me a half-smile. "No, sweetheart. That's for the whole time."

"We'll do it," I said. I didn't know how far a dollar thirty went, but it would probably buy us dinner if we weren't fussy.

"Fine. Sign these papers." She pushed one-page contracts across the table and gave each of us a pen. "I'm Molly Mallone, by the way. The star of the film."

"We don't have ID," I said carefully.

"We lost our bags on the train," Adeline added. Then she frowned for emphasis. "Stolen."

"It's fine." Molly lit a cigarette and blew a long plume of smoke into the air. "You just have to stand around while the cameras roll. The producers don't care. There's a tent set up in an empty lot." Molly recited the address. "Be there at 2:00 p.m. on the dot."

We smiled and thanked her. Neither of us knew what time it was, so we figured we'd just head on over there.

"Don't you find it odd that the star of the film is recruiting extras?" I asked.

"Yeah," Adeline said. "I'm sure it's a B movie."

We arrived at the big white tent and almost shouted for joy when we saw a table with drinks and finger sandwiches.

We handed our sign-up sheets to the guy at the entrance. He grinned and welcomed us to the team. We immediately headed for the food and ate as much as we could without attracting attention. I wished I'd thought to take a purse from the drama room, so I could store some food for later.

Molly arrived shortly after. She'd added a white hat to her look with a long feather sticking out of the black band. An extra layer of skirting hung over her waist with a sparkly clip holding it up at the hip. She fingered her strand of pearls as she shimmied up to a broad-shouldered guy who appeared to be in his late twenties. He wore a cream-color suit over a white shirt with the top two buttons undone.

"Hi, Mr. Vance," Molly purred.

"Hello, doll," the guy said. "I see you made good on your promise to find me extras on short notice."

"Say, I told ya, you can count on me."

Molly spotted us and approached. "I was afraid you would get lost, being visitors and all. Some folks sign up, all excited to be in a movie, but then... " She leaned closer and lowered her voice, "Because I know the pays not great, they change their minds."

"We don't mind," I said.

"Well, the Vance brothers know how to feed ya here," she said with a glint of admiration in her eyes. "That's for sure."

As delicately as I could, I wiped my mouth with my fingers. Did I have sandwich crumbs on my face?

"Brothers?" Adeline asked. "There's more than one?"

"Oh, yeah," Molly said. She looked happy to be able to enlighten us. That there is Sheldon, and Spenser should arrive shortly. There's another, the eldest son who lives on the east coast called Sylvester." She leaned in and whispered, "Some folks think the brothers are in dirty money."

Sheldon Vance was a dapper guy with Hollywood good looks. "Is he in the movie?" I asked.

"He mentioned a cameo part," Molly said. "I actually haven't met my leading man. The whole thing is really hush, hush. Mr. Vance said we're doing something brand new in film and he didn't want the competition to get wind of it. He hired me because I assured him I was good with improvisation."

I glanced over at Sheldon Vance and was shocked to find him looking at me. Did he hear us talking about him? Before I could avert my eyes, he nodded in acknowledgement and headed toward us.

"He's coming over," I whispered.

"Who?" Adeline said.

"Sheldon Vance."

Sheldon Vance cast a shadow over us before I could say more. His dark hair was shaved close around his ears and neck, but longer on top with bangs that hung over a tall forehead. His brown eyes were graced with striking, thick dark brows, which furrowed as he considered Adeline and me. There was something about his presence that was intimidating. Finally, the stony look on his face softened, and he cracked a smile.

"Hello, ladies," he said, extending a hand. "Welcome to my movie."

THIRTEEN

Sheldon Vance extended his hand. "Miss?"

"Donovan," I said. "But you can call me Casey."

Sheldon's grin tightened. "A pleasure to meet you Miss Casey Donovan."

He took Adeline's hand next and she answered, "Adeline Savoy."

My gut said not to trust this guy, but we didn't really have any choice. Not if we wanted to eat again, beyond a couple of small sandwich triangles.

A second man entered the tent, and Sheldon excused himself to greet him. The new guy was slighter in build, but I could see the resemblance in their dark eyes and thick brows.

"Spenser?" I asked Molly.

"Oh, yes. That's him." She played with her pearls, whirling them in a circle. "That means things are going to get started soon."

Sheldon Vance clapped his hands to get everyone's attention and spoke loudly. "Welcome everyone. Thank you for your willingness to participate in a new motion picture technique. Shortly we will be filming on location at Pacific Bank. Our film and lighting crew are there already and the stage is being set for a bank robbery. Though the bank is a real establishment, it is currently closed for business. The bank staff and customers there are hired actors. Molly has recruited you to be extras in the scene."

"But I thought I was the lead?" Molly whimpered.

Sheldon Vance's eyes flashed with momentary irritation before they softened again. "You are sweetheart. You'll be front and center, I promise."

"I guess it's just come as you are?" I asked. I didn't see any costume people.

"You lovely ladies may remain as you are. You're there to fill up the empty spaces as the scene calls for a busy day at the bank." He waved an arm toward Spenser Vance. "All the men are to see my brother for costumes."

Spenser Vance opened up a large canvas bag and pulled out black onesies, simple, plain and oversized. The guys, including Sheldon and Spenser, pulled them on over their clothes. Then our small crowd of extras followed Sheldon out of the tent to an automobile parked on the curb. Sheldon opened a long narrow suitcase and we all gasped when we saw the guns there. "Don't worry. These are only props." He handed one to his brother, and a couple to a few other hefty-looking guys. Then the Vance brothers drove off with their camera men in a car that had Vee Bros. Productions written on the side. The rest of us had to walk, and we followed Molly to the filming site. The air was warm and smelled of jasmine and hyacinths. A scattering of clouds marred the blue sky.

"Have you ever acted before?" I asked Adeline. "I know your dad does some work, but how about you?"

Adeline shook her head. "No. Every other student at Hollywood High has some kind of acting or film industry aspiration, but that's not me."

"What do you want to do?"

"I'm not sure." She cut a knowing look my way. "Our choices are limited, aren't they?"

"Yes. Which is why I'm going to be a writer. You can't do a whole lot of damage in a room by yourself."

"But can you make a living?" Adeline asked. "I've considered that option, too, but I don't think I have the writing chops. At least not to go the distance."

"It's a tough business. I think the key is being versatile. You have to be good at a lot of different kinds of writing."

"And disciplined," Adeline added. "I don't think I have the discipline required to be self-employed or work free-lance. Unless it's journalism. I'm more of a nonfiction type of gal."

"Journalism would be interesting," I added. "Or broad-casting."

"Radio, not TV," Adeline said.

I laughed. "TV could be disastrous."

"You're in the middle of a report, all cleaned up and rested, and the next second you're standing there with a drenched head or a black eye..." Adeline giggled. "I'd go for one of those late-night radio host jobs where you talk to insomniacs and play eighties rock."

We stood across the street from Pacific Bank. It was a one-story building with a barbershop on one side and a news-paper shop on the other. The Vee Bros. car was parked near the front door and the cameramen had their gigantic cameras poised on wooden stands, ready to roll.

"All the girls have to do," Molly said loud enough for the whole group to hear, "is walk inside and stand in a line. Chat with each other like you normally would. But whatever you do, don't look at the cameras. Guys, you get to play the robbers."

A testosterone-fuelled grunt rose from the male actors. I leaned into Adeline. "Talk about gender stereotyping."

We walked across the street, and I had to adjust my headband to keep it from sliding into my eyes.

We stopped in front of the Vance bros. camera crew. Sheldon Vance eyed me with his dark eyes and then his gaze landed on Adeline. Something about him gave me the creeps, and I stiffened to keep from shuddering in front of him.

"Here," he said, shoving a gun into my hand. "It's not loaded." He handed one to Adeline. "You dames come in behind me and Spenser."

Seems Sheldon was an equal opportunist after all.

"What about me?" Molly whined. "I thought I was the lead."

Sheldon handed her a gun, too. "Of course, doll. You go in first."

She giggled flirtatiously. "Do I have a line?"

"Yes, Molly. You say 'We're robbing this bank. Put your hands in the air.'"

"We're robbing this bank," she recited. "Put your hands in the air."

She turned to Adeline and me and spoke with authority. "It's just for effect. This isn't a talkie."

Everyone else was instructed to go in before us and

mingle with the actors already on set. "Get in line," Sheldon said. "Chat with your neighbor like you normally would."

After the brightness of the outdoors, it took a moment to get used to the dim lights. It looked like a regular banking day, with women in their shapeless dresses and men in crisp shirts and ties.

Sheldon and Spenser put stockings over their faces before handing out a few more to some of the other guys dressed in black. It was a good effect. They definitely looked sinister.

Sheldon gave Molly a countdown and she pushed through the doors with the Vance brothers, with Adeline and I on her heels. We all had our guns pointed.

"This is a bank robbery!" Molly said. "Put your hands in the air!"

Sheldon looked at her with distain. "Louder!"

I glanced at Adeline with bewilderment. I thought this was a silent film. Molly seemed equally confused, but then shouted, "THIS IS A BANK ROBBERY! PUT YOUR HANDS IN THE AIR!"

There were a few gasps and a lot of stunned faces. The small group that we had come with weren't as convincing as the others who were here before us. They must be professional actors.

"Quiet!" Sheldon said, scooting in front of Molly. "Do as the lady asked ya! Especially you fellas behind the counter."

Everyone's hands were up high. Spenser Vance, who'd let his brother do all the talking so far, went to the closest teller and pointed his gun right in his face. He was a thin man in his forties with a pencil mustache. His eyes were wide with fright, and his skin pale with fear. Sheldon gave him a bag. "To the top with hundreds."

I pointed my gun and ad-libbed. "Do as he says, mister."

Spenser Vance cut me a look, and I wondered if I'd overstepped. Adeline and I would have to search the archives for this movie, whatever it was called, when we got back. Though, with the shoddy production, it probably never got made. In fact, the whole thing seemed strange to me as I took it all in. I expected to see a lighting crew of some kind at work, a director or script person, but the bank was curiously devoid of behind-the-scenes people.

Something wasn't right with this scenario, but then again, I had no idea how things were done in this era. Movie production was very rudimentary.

Spenser backed away with his full sack while Sheldon guarded him and his haul. I wasn't sure what I was supposed to do. I looked to Molly for guidance, but she seemed just as confused. Adeline gave me a slight shoulder shrug.

The teller who'd filled Spenser's bag ran like a Weeble toward a side door. A gunshot reverberated in the room, and I ducked instinctively. What the hay? A red splotch appeared on the man's shoulder before he fell to the floor. One of the men dressed in black with hose over his head lowered a gun. He saw me watching and I could tell it was Sheldon even with the disguise. Pantyhose couldn't hide those brows.

I waited for someone to call, "cut," but instead I heard sirens in the distance. I wondered if they were sound effects and part of the scene. Then I remembered this was a "silent" film. The blood mark spreading along the teller's shirt looked awfully real. I heard the Vance jalopy fire up and glanced out the window in time to spot it zoom off out of sight. I searched the bank for Sheldon and Spenser, but none of the guys with face disguises were left in the room.

"Adeline?" I said with dread creeping up my spine. Her eyes widened with understanding.

"We need to get out of here!" She ran for the entrance, but it was too late. Several police stormed in, and one with a bullhorn shouted, "On the floor, everyone! Hands behind your heads!"

They looked like the real deal, not some wanna-be actors. A black wave of awareness that we had just screwed up big time washed over me. The police were dressed in black uniforms, a suit jacket fastened shut with a single row of gold buttons over a white shirt and black tie. They wore wide-brimmed hats. One of them aimed a pistol at Adeline and me—I guess the guns in our hands were a giveaway—and shouted, "Get down!"

I blurted out. "This is a big mistake!"

"Get down, now!"

My knees gave way and I lowered myself to the floor. The beads of my necklace poked my ribs. I press my palms against the back of my head and stared wildly at Adeline who lay beside me. She mouthed, "No way."

I felt the tip of a baton press into the middle of my back. A gruff voice said, "Don't move little lady." Rough hands grabbed my wrists and snapped metal handcuffs around them.

Handcuffs!

"I thought it was a movie," I whimpered.

"Uh-huh," he said as he toed my gun, pushing it out of reach.

"That's a prop."

He grunted. "Looks real enough to me."

One of the tellers, the thin man with a pencil-thin mustache who filled Sheldon's sack, pointed at me. "She was with them. She shouted at me to 'do as the man says,' and give him the money."

"I was *acting*. I didn't think it was real!"

The policeman shook his head incredulously. "Save it for the judge, miss."

We didn't even get the dignity of anonymity by riding in the back of a police jalopy. The police station was only three blocks away. I had to admire Sheldon's nerve to stage a robbery right under their noses.

The officer prodded Adeline and me down the sidewalk, and we lumbered along like cattle.

"I hope they catch those Vance brothers," Adeline said with spite.

"Me, too!"

Our chaperone scolded us. "No talking!"

I sighed and kept my head down. Now would be a really good time to trip home, and I wouldn't even care if I gave this cop a story he'd be telling for the rest of his life. But unfortunately, I didn't have control over when tripping through time happened, and it never happened when I wanted it to.

FOURTEEN

"Well, this sucks," Adeline said.

We both examined the sticky bench in the holding cell with disgust.

"I think I'll stand," I said.

Adeline crossed her arms. "Uh, yeah."

I fussed with my costume. There was a tear along one side seam, and it was dirty down the front from lying on the floor of the bank. I tried brushing it off, but it was stained. Adeline leaned against the wall and I joined her, though the wall wasn't exactly clean either. I wrinkled my nose. The room smelled *used*: sweat, stale air, and whatever was on that bench.

"I can't believe we fell for that," Adeline said. Her lips were pursed tight with frustration, anger maybe. "What are we going to do now?"

"I don't know," I said. As far as the authorities were concerned, Adeline and I had attempted a bank robbery. All the real—not acting—tellers had testified to that fact. And I stupidly called out, "Do as the man says, mister!" Ugh, way to implicate myself.

Molly Mallone had been taken elsewhere, the hospital maybe. She bawled like a baby when the police escorted her into the station, her legs limp as she gave into hysteria and shouted out her innocence. I wouldn't be surprised if she was happily sedated somewhere.

I was exhausted and my gaze landed on the bench once more. I really wanted to sit down, but not on that. Then I remembered I still wore my blouse and skirt under the flapper dress. I started to awkwardly wriggle them off while keeping the dress on.

Adeline eyed me with concern. "What are you doing?"

"We can sit on these," I said as I waved my twenty-first century clothes like a victory flag. I gave her my blouse then I laid my skirt on the bench and sat on it with a satisfied sigh.

Adeline positioned my blouse on the bench and sat beside me. "Have you ever been in jail before?"

I stared out at the black bars in front of us and shook my head. "No, but I had a few close calls. You?"

Adeline grinned. "Sort of. I was picked up in 1955 for indecent exposure." She snorted. "I went back while wearing a string bikini." She leaned her head back and closed her eyes. "They didn't put me behind bars, though."

We grew silent. There were some muffled sounds coming from the office around the corner. The clerk and secretary had seemed rather startled by our arrival, and I wondered how many arrests happened in small-town Hollywood in 1929.

Adeline broke our silence. "Why are you here?"

I glanced at her in confusion. "Because I allegedly robbed a bank?"

"No, I mean, what triggered your trip?"

"Oh." My heart pattered with renewed mortification and embarrassment, but before I could answer, she continued in a strained voice.

"I'm here because Marco and I had a fight."

"Really? You guys looked so happy when you introduced me." I remembered seeing them in a tense conversation later on though, but I didn't want to say that.

"We are happy most of the time."

"What happened?"

She grimaced. "I told him about..." She waved a hand through the air. "This. My travelling life."

"At the party?"

"Well, I was actually inspired by you. Your boyfriend knows all about you. I felt like I was keeping this big secret from Marco, and we've been together for a long time now. I need him to believe me.

"But, at the party?" I said again. This was a subject better suited for a private conversation, in my opinion.

"I know. It was stupid."

"What did he say?"

"He laughed it off. That's how he always deals with things he doesn't care about. That made me mad. The more I tried to explain it, the more he refused to talk about it. I asked him if he thought I was lying, and he hedged before saying 'not intentionally.' Then I was really mad. 'You think I'm crazy?' I said. It just got out of control so quickly."

"Well, it is hard to believe at first, you know, for people who've never gone back. Even when they do, it's hard for them to believe. It took Nate two days *living and breathing* in 1860 before he believed me."

Adeline adjusted the black hat on her head and sighed. "You're right. It was dumb of me to think he'd just say, 'Oh, cool. Can you take me sometime?'"

My hair had come loose from the kerfuffle. I pulled on a strand, unsure of what I should do. Take all the pins out?

Adeline noticed. "Let me fix that for you."

I turned my back to her and let her play with my hair. "Well," I began, "if it makes you feel any better, I screwed up way more than you."

"Yeah? How so?"

"I kissed another guy."

Her hands stopped, and I felt her stiffen in surprise. "What?"

I pressed my palms against my face as new regret washed over me. "This guy in my group, Austin, has been after me, you know, even though I repeatedly told him I had a boyfriend. Nate and I have been going through some things. He's gone a lot, and we haven't been communicating, and there's this girl who wants him, and she posted a picture of her all over Nate at a party, kissing him on the cheek, and I was so hurt, and Austin was there, and he put his arm around me to comfort me, and the next thing I knew, we're kissing!"

"Whoa, Nelly, take a breath," Adeline said.

"But I cheated!"

"Sounds like Nate cheated, too."

"Oh, Adeline, it's such a mess!" I felt the tears come, and I wiped at my face in a desperate attempt at dignity.

Adeline put in the last pin. "All done." Then she leaned against the wall and said, "I'm going to break up with him."

I spun to face her "What? Why?"

She sighed. "I really like Marco. He's a good guy, but I don't think we meant to go the distance, you know? Graduation is around the corner and Marco's going to college in San Diego. Look how hard it is for you and Nate to do the long-distance thing and he *knows* you."

I patted her knee. "You don't have to make a big decision like that now. Wait until we get back and you have some time to sleep on it."

"You're right, Casey." Her stomach chose that moment to rumble. "I'm starving."

"Me, too." It had been several hours since those tiny sandwiches. "I'd die for a bowl of my mom's beef stew right now."

Adeline blinked. "What's your mom like?"

"She's nice. Creative. Runs her own interior design biz."

"Does she look like you?"

"No. She's shorter by half a foot and blond." I tugged on a loose strand of my hair. "Not a curl in sight." I remembered how hard she fought to find Tim last summer, and how she took care of us when Dad was gone. "She's a good mom."

Adeline smiled, but her eyes flashed with sadness. "What about your mom?" I asked. "Is she a good cook?"

"She died when I was ten."

"Oh. I'm sorry." I just assumed she had two parents, but now that I thought about it, she only ever talked about her dad.

"It's okay. It's been a long time now."

"Do you remember her?"

"A little. I have pictures. We look a lot alike."

I didn't know what else to say, so I let the silence

surround us. Well, not silence exactly. The din of office voices grew increasingly louder until there was full-out yelling.

Before I saw anything, I heard the shuffling of bodies and dragging feet scraping along the linoleum. I stood and peered through the bars the best I could without touching them.

A man shouted, "You got nothin' on me! It's my word against his!"

I saw two scrawny police officers struggling to subdue one younger, well-dressed man. The man's eyes locked with mine before the police wrestled him down the hall and out of sight.

There was no mistaking those eyebrows.

Sheldon Vance.

His dark eyes were so steely and calculating, it made my blood ripple.

"He's scary," Adeline said.

I totally agreed. I felt dizzy and it took me a moment to register that it wasn't from a lack of food or the sudden realization that we had aided and abetted a man like Sheldon Vance, a man whose family, I had no doubt, was involved in "dirty money" as Molly claimed.

If the law found Adeline and me guilty of involvement with the Vance family, we were in big trouble.

I couldn't breathe.

I reached for Adeline's hand. "Hold on," I said. "We're going home."

Then we spiraled through a tunnel of bright light.

FIFTEEN

Why do I always forget where I came from when I travel back to my present? Panic gripped my chest when I was suddenly underwater. My eyes burned from the chlorine as I frantically pushed off the bottom of the deep end of the pool toward the surface. I gasped and sputtered when my face broke the surface.

"Are you guys okay?" Marco was bent at the knees at the edge of the pool. He reached out a hand to help Adeline out. Another arm reached for me, and I looked up to see Austin. Right. In his world, we'd just kissed, and I'd ran away and fell into the pool.

"Hey," he said. "That was quite the performance."

"I'm looking at a career in synchronized swimming."

"Well..." He grinned. "You're nailing it, though I think there are special costumes for that called swimming suits."

"Ah, I knew I was missing something."

Someone tossed us each a towel, and I wrapped mine around me. I had on my skirt and blouse, the very ones

Adeline and I had been sitting on in the jailhouse just moments before. Austin stared at me, and I could only imagine how terrible I looked. My hair was a tangled mess of wet curls, and I knew my eyes had the signature dark circles that came with the trip home. My clothes stuck to my body. I pulled on my shirt and attempted to wring the water free. Austin watched me the whole time. I felt self-conscious under his gaze and looked away.

"Adeline," I called. "Where's the bathroom?"

"This way." She began walking, and I followed her wet prints left behind on the tile. "They have robes for guests when they swim, so we can put our clothes in the dryer."

The staff was appalled by our topple into the family pool, and one of the maids ushered us to a large bathroom that had two toilet stalls, like a restaurant, and a door leading to the laundry room. She handed us the robes. She spoke with a strong Latina accent. "Leave your wet things in the basket, and I'll put them in the dryer for you. Is there anything else you need?"

"My purse?" Adeline said. " I left it on the patio. Marco will know which one it is."

Bluebell's maid knew Marco. I didn't think it would be fair to send her on a hunt for my pack, so I just shook my head. I had to trust Misha to watch it for me.

We stripped down and covered our wet bodies with the thick lush robes. "These are nice," I said.

I looked in the mirror at my raccoon eyes and helped myself to hand lotion, using a tissue to remove my makeup. Adeline did the same, uncovering the dark circles around her eyes as well.

The maid returned with Adeline's purse, and Adeline

removed a small satchel. "Make up," she announced. "We may have to go out there in robes, but we don't have to look like wet dogs."

It took us at least thirty minutes to recover and make ourselves look presentable. Adeline presented me with a handful of lipsticks to choose from. "Help yourself."

"I'm fine," I said, but I did borrow her mascara and eyeliner. I had lip gloss in my pack.

There was a round of applause for us when we returned. Adeline made a dramatic entrance like she was a returning queen. I was happy to stay in her wake. The way she and Marco embraced, I believed their fight was over for now and that she'd had a change of heart about breaking up with him. He was headed for a good shock one day when he finally tripped back with her, but I really sensed he was the type of guy who could handle Adeline's double life when he saw it for himself.

Misha approached me with my pack and we occupied two empty lounge chairs. "You must be so embarrassed," she said. "It did liven up the party though."

I wasn't sure how to respond to that. I fished for my lip gloss and put it on. "I'm really tired," I said to her. "I hope we go back to the hostel soon."

"Are you kidding!" She flicked her honey-blond hair over her shoulder and pressed up on her glasses. "It's early. And we're in Hollywood! We can't sleep our time here away."

I was glad one of us was having a good time. Misha skipped away and her vacancy was soon filled by Austin. Of course. He sat sideways on the lounge chair and faced me.

His blond brows danced. "You know how to rock a robe."

I blinked, unsure of myself and how I should now

behave. I clearly remembered our kiss, his lips on mine, and I swallowed hard.

His tongue dampened his bottom lip and he stared at me like he was remembering, too.

Oh my goodness!

He tilted his head and eyed me with concern. "Are you okay?"

"Uh, yeah, sure." *Why wouldn't I be???*

"Good." He stretched out on the lounge chair, putting his hands behind his head. "This party turned out to be way more fun than I thought it would be." He closed his eyes and a small smile tugged on his face. "First a kiss, then a wet T-shirt contest."

I slapped his arm. "Shut up!"

"Ow!" he feigned pain, then laughed out loud.

My phone rang. I thought it might be Mom or Lucinda, but my heart jumped when I saw Nate's face appear on the screen. I quickly accepted the video call.

"Hey," he said. "I can only talk for a couple minutes, but I wanted to see you." He missed me! And he looked good. His grin turned upside down. "Where are you?"

I turned my back to Austin. "At a pool party."

"What are you wearing?"

Oh, right. "A robe. I fell in and got my clothes wet."

"You fell in?"

"Yeah."

His scowl deepened. "Is that King?"

What? I looked over my shoulder to see that Austin had moved in close behind me. I pushed him back, out of view.

"Casey? What's going on? Are you *with* him."

"No. No! It's nothing. I just..."

It was so unlike Nate to jump to conclusions like that.

Unless.

Unless he had a guilty conscience!

"What about you and—"

The screen went black. The call dropped. I pushed reply, but couldn't get through. Oh, no. Could this day get any worse? Ugh!

SIXTEEN

Austin had hunter instincts and managed to step inside my comfort zone on more than one occasion over the next two days, but I used Adeline and Misha as shields to keep him away.

The radio silence with Nate continued throughout the weekend, and I literally felt sick with apprehension. My stomach had its own beach party going on and food wasn't invited. I forced myself to eat anyway, and knowing I wasn't enjoying the California cuisine as much as I should be felt like a fitting punishment.

Mr. Ryerson kept our group busy, and Adeline and I only had time on Sunday afternoon to grab a quick mocha at one of the many Starbucks.

"Still nothing from Nate?" Adeline asked. It was so nice to have a friend here to talk to about this. Normally, I'd chat into the early hours of the morning about boy problems with Lucinda, but I used my busyness here as an excuse not to call her. The real reason was that I was embarrassed by my bad behavior with Austin. It was so unlike me. I couldn't account for it.

"He's still unreachable," I said with a pout. "The time difference and his game schedule make it nearly impossible and it's driving me crazy to have this...thing between us." I blew on my coffee. "I can't believe he jumped to conclusions about Austin like that!"

Adeline tilted her head and considered me kindly. "And yet, he was right, sort of."

"The kiss was a mistake!"

"Are you going to tell him about it?"

My stomach flip-flopped. "I don't want to, but I know I probably should."

"Why?" Adeline leaned in closer. "It didn't mean anything, and Austin obviously took advantage of you. Anyone can see he's after you."

"He is, right?"

She sat back and pushed blond strands behind her ears. "And what Nate doesn't know won't hurt him."

I nodded, but I wasn't sure that was true. "I just can't wait until everything gets back to normal between us."

I checked the time on my phone. We only had a short while before I had to return to my group. It was Adeline's turn to moan about her man. "What about you and Marco?" I asked. "Did you tell him about our latest trip?"

She frowned and shook her head. "The opportunity hasn't presented itself. I'm not even sure what to say to him now. Last time, I told him I traveled to the fifties. Do I now change my story to the twenties? And where will I go next time?"

I had the same question. Though life in the twenties was

more modern than the nineteenth century and I didn't have to worry about Civil War issues, the stock-market crash was imminent, and then I'd be dealing with The Great Depression and eventually World War II.

Neither timeframe was great, but at least in 1863, I had the Watson family. I'd hated the thought that I might never see them again.

"Besides," she continued, "it's all moot if we don't stay together."

MONDAY MORNING ROLLED AROUND, and it was time to say good-bye to our new friends, who, along with Ms. Bianco, had walked over to our hostel to see us off. We hugged and (some of us) shook hands before boarding the airport shuttle bus. Adeline and I swapped phones and we added each other to our contacts.

"I'm so glad we met up again," I said. It was a happy serendipitous event.

"Me too." Adeline grinned widely. "And those extra bonus days..."

I laughed. "Were a bonus!"

That was the thing about tripping. No matter how many days you lived through while visiting the past, you got them back on the return.

Mr. Ryerson gave us the times-up signal and told us to start boarding the shuttle. I gave Adeline an extra-long squeeze. "Keep in touch," I said.

Once we got to the airport, I spoke with Mr. Ryerson to confirm that Austin *wasn't* sitting next to me on the trip back. He assured me that Misha had the seat next to me, and I had the window seat as requested.

"I'm going to be sleeping the whole way back," I warned Misha, "so I won't be much for company."

"Didn't you sleep well last night?"

I hadn't. My thoughts kept going to Nate and all I had to tell him. Austin and the kiss. Tripping with Adeline. Robbing a bank.

"I'm not great with flying," I responded. "It's just better if I don't remember it at all."

Misha gave me a curious look then adjusted her glasses and returned to the book she was reading on her phone.

Soon after, the flight attendant called for boarding. I found my seat and swallowed the last two pills. I propped my pillow against the window, watched as the plane taxied to the runway, and said good-bye to the sunny, smoggy skies of LA before closing my eyes and drifting to sleep. Next thing I knew, Misha was shaking my shoulder.

"Wake up! We're in Boston."

I had bed-head and sleep in my eyes, but I was relieved to have made it back to Massachusetts. Now I knew I could fly short distances and live to tell about it, but I wasn't eager to do it again anytime soon.

Tim picked me up from the airport. I made a point of saying good-bye to everyone except Austin, pointedly ignoring him before crawling into Tim's beat-up Cavalier.

He punched me playfully in the shoulder. "Good to see you alive and in one piece."

I punched him back. "I told you I'd be fine."

"Yeah, well, I'd appreciate it if you didn't fly again

anytime soon." Then as an afterthought, he added, "Nothing happened...did it?"

I stared out the window so he couldn't see the expression of guilt on my face. "What do you mean?"

"I mean, did you visit California in the year of our Lord 1863?"

"No, I didn't." It wasn't a lie and I didn't feel the need to fill him in on the whole truth. It was over. I'm of sound body if not sound mind. Why worry him for nothing?

Mom and Dad were both gone when I got home, so I texted them to let them know I was back and okay. I unpacked, which basically meant dumping the contents of my suitcase into the laundry, and checked my e-mail hoping for something from Nate. Long-distance dating sucked big time. I hated that I couldn't just call him, or that my only line to my boyfriend's life was the updates on the BU website that I was busy scrolling.

I smiled at the shots of the team in action and zoomed in on Nate's face. My heart ached. I missed him.

Of course there were plenty shots of the cheerleaders too, and Fiona's Latino glam was hard to miss.

She must've remembered to buy a proper phone plan because her Facebook page was full of photos uploaded from Spain. They'd had time to sight-see over the weekend, and there were plenty of shots of Barcelona's landmarks. Somehow Nate was always in them. Sometimes, he was looking away, but often he was smiling at the camera. At Fiona. Besides the first set of her getting chummy with Nate, there weren't any others with them hanging on each other, though I doubted she'd be stupid enough to post any of them kissing, if they did kiss.

Oh, man, I hope they hadn't. I don't know what I would do if Nate cheated on me with her.

I was such a hypocrite!

Only three more days and Nate would be back. We could put this whole craziness behind us. Move on from Fiona and Austin.

My phone beeped. I grabbed it and squealed.

Nate: *Can't wait to get home and see you. Sorry about overreacting the other day. Won't ever forget to buy a phone plan again!*

My belly filled with gooey happiness. I ignored the inference that Nate would be traveling around the world without me again in the future, and focused on the part were he couldn't wait to see me.

My phone beeped again, and I smiled, anticipating another text from Nate.

It was Lucinda, and I reigned in my disappointment. I missed my best friend and had planned to connect with her next. I frowned at her text.

Lucinda: *Have you seen this? Looks like YOU had a good time. Must talk soon.*

She posted a picture. It was from the pool party at Bluebell's mansion. A profile shot of Austin and me lip-locking.

Oh, no.

SEVENTEEN

Lucinda and I had been best friends since we were eight years old. I accidentally took her back in time when we were ten, and to say she had been traumatized by the experience would be an understatement. She couldn't even look at me for a week at school and when I did manage to catch her dark brown eyes, they flashed with fear.

Eventually, she warmed up to me again, and her fear was overshadowed by empathy. As long as she didn't touch me, she was safe. Our friendship grew over the years. We watched movies on weekends, did homework while eating pizza, and as we got older, boy-watched from the sidelines. We were both happy in our awkward middle-school years since we had each other and didn't mind staying on the peripheral of the social scene, a status that continued when we became freshmen in high school.

Lucinda had been a faithful keeper of my secret for years, and because of this, I told her everything. Besides my brother and my boyfriend who'd only discovered my "gift" in the last couple years, she was the only other person who knew about my propensity to fall back in time. She was my only friend who knew.

Until now, with Adeline.

Lucinda was a great friend, but that didn't make her a perfect person, and one flaw she did have was a tendency toward jealousy if she felt her position as my BFF was being threatened. It took her a while to accept Nate when he came into my life, and it was only when she started having her own boyfriends that he became a non-issue for her.

I'd been home from Hollywood for three days, and I still hadn't told her about the trip to the twenties, mainly because I didn't want to tell her how I'd somehow changed my time loop, because to do that, I'd have to bring up Adeline, and I didn't want to do that if I didn't have to.

We *had* discussed in depth my short but devastating kissing session with Austin King.

"He keeps staring at you," Lucinda said as we sat at our usual table in the cafeteria.

My heart jittered at her words. "Just ignore him."

She snorted. "He's going to drill a hole in the back of your head with his gaze."

My phone buzzed before I had a chance to respond, and I was glad for the distraction. It was Adeline texting.

Our time in the twenties had been a bonding experience and we'd been messaging each other a couple times a day since. Neither of us had ever met anyone who truly understood the challenges we faced on a daily basis. How acute our senses had to be when we traveled back just to survive and how sometimes they just were not acute enough and you still ended up in jail.

Casey: Have you tripped since?

Adeline: No, thank goodness.

Casey: Me neither.

Adeline: Though I'm curious if I'll reset back to the fifties or if it's the twenties for good.

Casey: That's what I want to know!

Adeline: Have you worked things out with Nate?

Casey: Not yet. He gets home today. I'm excited and nervous.

"Who are you talking to?"

My head jerked up at Lucinda's voice. "Oh." I couldn't out and out lie to her, so I tried for vague. "This girl I met in Hollywood."

Lucinda flicked her straight dark hair over her shoulder. "What's her name?"

I hesitated. "Adeline." Why couldn't she have a super common name like Sarah or Jessica. Lucinda always had a brain for details, and I knew she'd remember.

She cocked her head. "Wasn't that the name of that girl you met once, who said she was also a traveler?"

I nodded, not breaking our gaze. Lucinda blinked and her face hardened. "And you didn't think to tell me?"

"I was going to, it's just, a lot more happened than trips to Universal Studios and the wax museum."

"Isn't that *more* reason to tell me?"

"I know, I was going to."

Lucinda's eyes narrowed at me. "Were you?"

My phone buzzed again and I checked the message.

Adeline: Marco wants to talk tonight. I think he's sensing I'm backing off. What should I do? I thought I was sure, but now I'm not so sure."

I glanced back up at Lucinda. "I'll tell you all about it, I promise. I just need to respond to this."

Lucinda scowled and picked up her tray. "You don't have to tell me, you know." Her words were laced with bitterness. "We're not married. If you want to keep this new friendship to yourself, and your Hollywood adventures a secret, that's fine with me."

The way she straightened her shoulders and left without looking back, I knew there was no way it was fine with her.

Casey: Get angry. That's your trigger, right? And take him back with you.

Adeline: LOL. That would freak him out so much!

Casey: But he'd have to believe you.

Adeline: I don't think I want him to believe me anymore. I'm going to end it tonight. :(

Casey: Oh, boo. I'm here if you need me.

A body shifted in beside me and I could tell by the arctic scent of his cologne that it was Austin. I stared at him, anger filling my gut at the bemused expression on his face.

"Why'd you do it?" I asked.

"Do what? Kiss you? I think you know the answer to that."

"No, why'd you send out that picture?" The kissing picture had circulated widely through the Cambridge High social network, and my only hope was that Nate was unable to get online in Spain to see it. For once I was thankful for his shoddy phone plan.

"If we break up over it," I added, "I'll never forgive you."

He looked taken aback. "What are you talking about? What picture?"

"The one of you kissing me."

His eyebrows jumped. "There's a picture of that? I'd like to see it."

"This isn't funny." I knew by the smirk on his face that he had seen it.

"I'd like to correct your description of said picture. You were kissing me."

I glared at him. "Semantics. Someone took that picture and posted it."

"Obviously, since I was in the picture, I didn't take it."

Obviously. "Who else would have anything to gain by sending that out?"

"Look, Casey, I'm not going to lie and say I didn't enjoy the kiss or that my heart would be broken if you and Mackenzie called it quits, but I didn't arrange for that picture to be taken and I didn't post it."

"If you didn't, then who did?"

"I don't know, but it appears that I'm not the only one interested in seeing you back on the market."

I smacked his arm. He laughed. "You're really cute when you're angry." He reached over and squeezed my shoulder. "See ya later, Donovan."

When I got home after school, my phone buzzed. A message from an unidentified sender. A photo. Austin and me in the school cafe. He was smiling down at me with his hand on my shoulder. My eyes were locked on his. You couldn't see the contempt in them. From this angle, we looked like we were flirting.

My face flushed with heat. Oh, God. Who was taking these photos?

EIGHTEEN

THE TERRIERS WERE HOME late Saturday night and I wasn't about to wait a moment longer than necessary to see Nate. First thing Sunday morning, I hopped the redline to Boston and practically jogged to the BU campus and to Nate's dorm. I tried to shake out my nerves on the elevator ride to the fourth floor. I walked quickly to his door, my heart tittering like a frightened mouse in a cage. I pinched my eyes together and knocked.

The door swung open and an angry-looking Nate stood on the other side. He'd recently showered since his hair was still damp and hung in waves around his face. He held up his phone.

"Look what I just got," he said with tight lips.

I didn't have to look. I knew. Whoever had just sent me the photo from the cafeteria had sent it to Nate, too.

"And it's not the only one." He swiped his finger across the face of his phone and presented the kissing picture.

"Nate, let me explain." I wanted to throw myself at him

and kiss him deeply on the lips, but he'd crossed his arms and leaned back against the open door.

"Please, can we talk?" I asked.

I could hear movement and turned to see Nate's two roommates. They threw me tentative chin nods, like they weren't sure if it was okay for them to greet me.

Nate grabbed his hoodie. "Let's take a walk."

The energy in the elevator was so tense you'd need a chainsaw to cut through it. Nate wouldn't even look at me. The bell dinged as the doors opened to the lobby and I followed Nate outside.

I was tall, but even so I found it hard to keep up with Nate's long strides. He shoved his fists into the pockets of his hoodie and stared straight ahead.

"This is all a big mistake," I said.

"The pictures look pretty convincing to me."

I stopped short. "Yeah? What about the pictures of you and Fiona? Everyone could see that you had hooked up. It was humiliating!"

Nate stopped finally, at least five feet ahead of me and turned. "Is that why you kissed King? You thought I was making out with Fiona?"

"No. Maybe. I was vulnerable and Austin..."

"Don't go blaming this on King. You only need half a brain to see you were all in on that kiss."

"I'd never kissed anyone but you before. He challenged me."

"What? You were *experimenting*?"

Why was this argument always turned back on to me? "What about Fiona?!"

"There are no pictures of me kissing Fiona because I

never kissed her! That display was all her. She wrapped herself around me, almost pushed me to the ground, and one of her friends took the picture. I extracted myself from her immediately."

The pain and anger that pinched Nate's face frightened me and I was awash anew with regret and shame. I'd jumped to conclusions and did the very thing I'd accused him of. *I was the cheater.*

I'd *cheated* on Nate. "I'm sorry. I don't know what got into me. Austin had been pressuring me all week, and then at the party, he showed me the photos of you and Fiona. He caught me at a weak moment."

Nate let out a long breath, and the pain of my betrayal emanated from him like shock waves. I felt my eyes water. "I'm so, so sorry, Nate. I was wrong to doubt you. Just, so much time has gone by since I saw you and then with your phone absence..."

"It's not an apology if you make it my fault."

Oh, God. I was screwing this up so badly. "It's not your fault! I know that. It's mine, all mine. I don't know what else to say except that I'm sorry."

His phone pinged, and he his eyes filled with fury when he checked the screen.

Whatever it was, it was bad, and I had a sinking feeling it had to do with me.

"What is it?" I squeaked.

He turned the screen to me and I gasped. It was a picture of me leaning against Austin on the plane!

"That's nothing!" I stammered. "I'd taken sleeping pills and fell asleep. I'm sleeping!"

"On his shoulder, Casey?"

"I meant to lean on the window, but the pills kicked in so fast."

I felt tears burn behind my eyes. *Who* was doing this?

"I promise you, Nate, I didn't even want to sit next to Austin. And that was on the way there. I double-checked with Mr. Ryerson that I didn't have a seat next to him on the way back."

Nate turned his back to me and started walking. "I need some time."

I couldn't let him leave. My heart pounded. I couldn't bear to lose him like this. I couldn't bear not to have him with me, to gaze on his face, even if he was angry and couldn't stand the sight of me. I skipped ahead and grabbed his hand. "Please, don't."

He didn't pull away in time. I was hit with a wall of dizziness and a flash of light. Instead of disappearing like it would had we traveled to 1863, the university still existed, only now the buildings had changed in size and position. Instead of horse-and-buggies, Model Ts rumbled down the street beside us, which was unpaved and without sidewalks.

"Casey?" Nate looked at me with wide questioning eyes. "What's going on?"

I swallowed. "It's been reset."

"Reset?"

"That's the only way I can explain it."

"To what year?" He seemed extraordinarily calm, but I knew him well enough to know that he was managing his anger.

"1929."

He scowled. "How?"

"Do you remember Adeline?"

Nate's eyes flickered. "I'm not sure."

"I met her before we started going out officially, at a convenience store near here. I saw her demeanor change in front of me, and she suddenly had dark circles under her eyes."

"Right. She was a traveler. Didn't she move to California?"

I nodded, and understanding came to Nate's eyes. "You met her there?"

"This freaky thing happened where we both tripped at the same time."

"Touching each other?" he asked incredulously.

"We were at a pool party. She'd just fought with her boyfriend, Marco, which triggered her trip, and I..."

Nate finished for me. "... just kissed Austin King."

"I was so upset by it, I ran off without looking where I was going. I ran into Adeline, and we fell into the pool."

"And now you trip to the *twenties*?" His face grew red. "This is terrible, Casey!"

I agreed, but I tried to soften it with faulty reasoning. "At least I don't have to worry about the Civil War."

"You also don't have the Watsons! You don't know Boston in the twenties. You don't have any friends here to help you!"

"I know that! You think I don't know that?"

We were arguing loudly, and our unconventional dress was garnering unwanted attention. The men were dressed in trousers and overcoats, not low-riding jeans and hoodies. The women wore dresses, fitted jackets and hats over short, bobbed hair. My hair, though pulled back in a ponytail, was a long curly mess and I wore jeans and a pink hoodie.

Nate took charge. "We have to find a place out of sight to hang out for awhile, until we can figure out our next move."

"Where?" I asked, feeling completely out of my element. At least Nate was somewhat familiar with the campus.

"I think I know where." He took my hand and I didn't let go. No matter what happened to us in our present, we needed each other to get back there.

The campus grounds were sparse in 1929. "I thought Boston U was established in the late 1800s," I said.

"It was, but the fire of 1872 forced the relocation to several buildings spread out over town." He ran a hand through his dark hair as he scanned the landscape.

Though the campus grounds were sparse, the city of Boston was not. Cars looked different from modern vehicles, but with narrow roads with rough pavement or old cobblestones, the congestion was just as thick. We headed toward an industrial section nearby and Nate pointed to a warehouse.

"There," he said. "That's a coffee shop and art gallery in our time."

A large sign along the front read, "Macmillan Textile Co. Ltd."

"It's a clothing factory," Nate said. "There are old pictures of this place hanging on the coffee shop walls. Rows of women bent over sewing machines."

I pulled on the front door, but it was locked. "It's closed," I said.

"It's Sunday. Everything will be closed." He rounded the corner toward the back of the building. I scouted the area to ensure we weren't spotted, then followed him.

Nate had to climb onto a large garbage bin to reach the

first row of high windows. He pushed against the pane with two palms. "I think I can get this open." He grunted and the glass slid up, just enough that a narrow body could squeeze through.

He bent over the bin and reached for my hand and pulled me onto the bin. "I'll go first," he said, "so I can help you down."

Nate jumped into the darkness, and my heart leaped into my throat. I straddled the windowsill and swung both of my legs inside. Nate reached for my waist and helped me down.

It was nice. I could've hopped to the cement floor on my own, and probably without twisting an ankle, but I was happy to have Nate touch me. He wasn't warm and affectionate. His aid was purely functionary. I wasn't sure where we stood anymore, if he still wanted to be my boyfriend. If he even still considered himself my boyfriend. Right now, in this moment, he was all business.

"I'm hoping there's some clothing available to us here," he said.

The room was vast, with many rows of sewing machines, just like Nate had described. The high windows allowed some daylight into the space, enough for us to make out what was in front of us without having to turn on the lights.

Many of the machines had fabric left in them, secured by the needle, as if the seamstress stopped where she was when the end of the day struck. There was a number of mannequins dotting the area with outfits draped on them. A closer inspection confirmed that the costumes were yet unfinished, partially sewn with some pieces pinned together.

"I could finish one of these," I said.

"You can sew?"

"I took home economics."

"So did I."

I couldn't hold in my surprise. "You did?"

"Guys need to know how to cook and sew, too," he said. "Twenty-first century women don't do it all for them anymore. Unfortunately." He said that last word with a grin, and it gave me hope that maybe he was thawing out. That maybe he would forgive me.

Nate found a nearly complete pair of trousers in one of the machines, and we both set to sewing. The machines were cumbersome and inefficient, and it was hard to make clean, straight stitches. I broke thread more than once and struggled to rethread the needle in the dim daylight. The peddle action took a little getting used to, but it meant we could sew without power.

It had grown dark by the time we finished.

"There must be bathrooms," I said. "We can change there."

We found the rooms at the back, and I pulled a string from a bulb in the ceiling to create light. The room had two stalls, not nearly enough for the number of women who obviously worked here, but at least there was indoor plumbing.

The dress I'd completed was a light blue satin with a darker blue band that hung low across the hips. There was no waist to speak of so the seams from under the arms to the hems were almost a straight line. Thankfully, the sleeves had been hand-stitched in place as a guide and I just had to follow.

It wasn't perfection, hanging a little crookedly, but it

would do. I removed my hair tie and created a new low bun at the base of my neck.

My bare face didn't fit in with this era, so I delved into a stray makeup bag, thankful to the girl who was probably kicking herself right now for leaving it at work on the weekend. I added dark smoky shadow, a black line of liner and mascara to my eyes. Red for my cheeks and lips and I was ready to rock this decade.

I met Nate in the hallway and he stopped short when he saw me, his jaw going slack. Then he grinned. "You look like a flapper."

"I hope so."

Nate was wearing the trousers with finished cuffs on the bottom. He was already wearing a button down shirt, which he'd tucked in.

"You look good," I said.

"Well, we still need proper shoes and jackets," he said.

I stared down at my sneakers. At least in 1863 a long dress could cover my shoes.

"I don't suppose there's any left behind in the mud room?" The workers had to hang up coats and leave boots somewhere, but they'd more than likely take them home, wouldn't they?

Just then we heard the creak of a door.

"Quick, turn out the lights," Nate whispered. I sprinted to the ladies room and pulled the string just as the light in the men's room went out. Back in the hall, Nate reached for me and led me by the elbow into the dark corner where I pressed up against him. I felt Nate's heart beat through my back and mine thudded in tandem. Was it the owner? Security? Perhaps the police drove by and saw a hint of light that escaped the bathrooms?

Whispered voices echoed through the foyer, bouncing off the tall ceilings.

"Oh, Roger, are you sure we won't get caught?"

Robbery? They were pretty loud for thieves.

"*Shh,*" Roger said. Then sounds like kissing. And giggles. They weren't here to rob the place, they were here to make out!

"There's a bed in the nurse's lounge." More laughing. "Give me your coat," he said. "You won't be needing that."

We stayed still in our dark corner until the giggling and smooching sounds disappeared and the door to the nurse's lounge clicked shut.

We tiptoed softly to the foyer and without speaking, slipped into the coats that hung on the hooks on the wall and the boots that lay askew on the floor, and headed quietly out the front door.

NINETEEN

"WHERE ARE WE GOING?" I asked.

This was a strange scenario for me. I used to be the seasoned one, the one who did the teaching and the leading, not the one who was taught and led. In the 1860s, I was the expert, but here in the twenties, I was green and inexperienced in every way. I was familiar with Boston in the present and in the nineteenth century, but this version, though it had a few similarities to each, was changed enough that I felt lost.

"I'm not sure," Nate said. "I wouldn't mind eating, and we need to find a place to sleep."

"Both of those things require money," I said.

His lips tightened. "They do."

So how did one make money on the fly in Boston, in March, 1929? I doubted there was a movie filming, so working as extras was out. And besides, I was no longer interested in acting gigs.

"We need to get downtown," Nate said. We heard a tram

approach, and his green eyes flickered with sentimentality. "You up for it again?"

I knew instantly that he was referring to the times when we hitched a ride on the back of buggies in the nineteenth century, or that time we had to run and hop a train.

"I am," I said.

Nate crossed to the other side, and when the trolley passed, we both ran to catch a bumper. I held on tight, crouching low so the folks on the tram, especially the ticket guy, wouldn't see us. It was growing darker but still light enough for some witnesses to shout and holler. I hoped they didn't draw the attention of a traffic cop.

I kept my eyes set on Nate, waiting for his signal to jump. He mouthed, "Now," and I lowered myself and broke into a run as my feet hit the ground to keep from tripping and face planting. I wasn't graceful, but I avoided tearing my dress or skinning my knees, which was a bonus.

Nate waved for me to cut through an alley to the next street and I scampered after him. I was surprised at how much construction there was. Boston was a boomtown in 1929. It seemed like everyone had money to burn. If only they could see into the future like Nate and I could. Their optimistic outlook was soon to come crashing down.

I still had to talk to Nate about what had happened in Hollywood. He'd jumped into his leader/protector role he often took with me, but the softness was gone from his eyes when he looked at me.

"Nate, I need to get back to why I came to see you today."

His paced picked up slightly. "I know why you came, Casey."

I tugged on his sleeve. "Please, can we talk about it?"

"Go ahead and talk." He didn't slow, so I kept my strides long to keep up with him, which was a little tough in this tube dress. I hiked up one side above my knees.

"That latest picture, it's not what it looks like."

He scoffed and challenged me. "What did it look like?"

"It looks like Austin and I are flirting, but we weren't. Well, maybe he was, but I was glaring at him and telling him to leave me alone. You just can't see that in the photo."

"Were you glaring at him in the one where you had your eyes closed and your lips attached to his?"

"I already explained that one to you, Nate. That was a stupid mistake. But these other photos, I don't know, it's like someone is trying to break us up."

"Like King, maybe?"

"Yes, him, for sure, but he obviously wasn't the one taking the photos."

"He's got someone in on the game."

"I thought so too, but then I talked to him—"

Nate stopped still. "You talked to him? I thought you said you were staying away from him?"

I didn't remember if I said that or not, but it didn't matter. Nate thought I did. "I was mad about the photos. I had to tell him to stop."

He huffed. "Doesn't look like he got the message."

"He's trying to break us up, Nate."

I know he heard me, but he wouldn't look me in the eye.

When Nate finally responded, he didn't say what I was hoping he would. That what we had was too precious to let someone like Austin break us up. That we'd just put it all behind us and remember that we loved each other. Instead, he said, "We need to find you a new family, a 1929 version of the Watsons."

I frowned. "It's not that easy. I stumbled onto the Watson farm, and it took years to get to the place where they considered me one of their own."

I choked on the realization that I probably would never see them again. They had become like a second family to me, especially Sara Watson, and as we made our way through the crowd of *this* Boston, I felt a new well of grief bubble up inside me.

Nate's keen interest in finding me a new family made me worry that he was looking for a way to hand me off. Wash his hands of his presumed responsibility.

I had to think of something else to focus on before I had an emotional breakdown. We still had the problem of no money.

"Maybe we could get work in a restaurant, washing dishes or something"

Nate grunted, "It's Sunday. Everything's closed."

"Everything can't be closed," I said. "Look at all the people out and about. They're dressed like they're going somewhere."

Nate slowed to consider this. "Let's follow them."

We caught up to a group of six, three couples, all dressed similarly to the way Nate and I were dressed. We kept our distance and watched as they disappeared down a stairwell near the front entrance of a brownstone townhouse. We heard music escape as the door opened and the group went in. The door closed firmly and the noise disappeared.

"I don't see any signs," I said. "Must be a private party."

"This is the prohibition era, right?" Nate said. "It could be a speakeasy."

"A speakeasy?"

"A club that sells alcohol."

I slowed. "Oh."

"Drinking and distributing alcohol was illegal in the twenties. The law just made people want to imbibe more than ever."

"We can't go in," I said. "We're underage."

"There's no age limit, Casey. It's illegal for all ages. But there's probably a way to score some cash inside."

Another group of four entered the stairwell. Nate pulled my arm and we stepped in behind them. Nate and I were both tall, and I had a ton of makeup on, so we must've looked old enough for the doorkeeper, because he didn't do anything to stop us from entering.

I was shocked by how crowded it was. Men and women of all ages smoking and drinking and dancing—there was barely room to get by and find an empty seat. As it was, most of the girls sat on the laps of the guys they came with. Nate managed to snag an empty chair. He smirked and patted his thigh. I sat on his lap and wrapped an arm around his neck. It was almost like everything was okay between us.

The beautiful young people were dressed to the nines: girls with shimmering dresses, cascading pearls and feathers in their hair, and guys swaggering about with peacock confidence. Smoke swirled about their faces and their breath was dire. They were like a swarm of attractive dragons. I choked back a cough.

I was probably the only one who noticed. Before too long, I'd become scent blind like the rest of them.

The music was lively, loud and jazzy. Lots of brass instruments, eclectic chords and mesmerizing drum beats. I couldn't stop my feet from tapping and my shoulders moved on their own accord.

"Let's dance!" I shouted, and tugged Nate to his feet. Dancing was how our long and winding romance had begun, after all, back when I was still a freshman at what had become the Fall Dance to Remember.

Nate stiffened. "Casey, we need to be serious."

"We can't be serious all the time. We need to have some fun, too."

I watched the dancers around us. I'd seen enough episodes of Dancing with the Stars to recognize the Charleston and the cha-cha. I flung my heels back and to the side with the beat and swiveled my hips until the layered fringes of my dress flew side to side. I laughed at the joy of it and Nate's smile of amusement was a big reward. If I could change his mood, maybe I could change his mind about me.

When the song ended, I collapsed into Nate's arms. "Admit it," I said. "That was fun!"

"Yeah, it was, but now I'm dying of thirst and have no money to buy a drink."

I frowned. Way to ruin the moment, Nate.

A waiter approached us with a tray filled with amber and clear liquid that I was quite certain was not juice or water. Nate shook his head and mouthed, no money.

The waiter's gaze narrowed and he pointed to the door. "No sense takin' up real estate then."

Before we could respond, another body crashed into us, and the waiter spilled a couple of his drinks. He cussed and hurried back to the bar.

A girl who looked to be in her twenties with a sandy blond bob made with perfectly coiffed finger waves giggled at us. Her eyes lingered for a moment on Nate. She giggled again. "Excuse me, it's just so busy."

"It's fine," I said. "You probably saved us from an embarrassing toss out onto the street."

"I heard. Hey, you're quite the Oliver Twist. We're short a chorus girl tonight and if you want to fill her spot, there's ten clams in it for ya."

I guessed Oliver Twist was slang for dancer and hoped clams meant dollars. I grinned and said, "Sure!"

"Hey, wait, Casey," Nate said. "What kind of dancing is it, anyway?"

I nudged him. "It'll be fine. This is the twenties. How bad can it be?"

"I'm Marlene," the girl said. "Follow me. We're up in fifteen."

I left with Marlene before Nate could stop me, getting lost in the crowded dance floor and through an exit to the left of the small stage where the band played.

"You and your fella new to Boston?" Marlene asked.

"Yes, well, we've been here before but it's been awhile."

"Lots of kids come to the city to find jobs. There's just no money in farming anymore."

The dressing room had rows of mirrors lined with round light bulbs. Marlene handed me a skimpy, glittery costume, like a gymnast would wear, but with a large fan of feathers attached to the butt. "You'll be in the back," she said, "so just follow along. It's mostly a lot of kicking our legs in the air." She laughed. "Doesn't take much to make the fellas happy and Mr. Vance thinks it's the berries."

I froze. "Mr. Vance?" I choked out.

Marlene's smile faltered. "Do you know him?"

"Uh, no. Of course not. Just thought I'd heard the name before."

"The Vance brothers are big eggs, so it's no wonder you've heard of them." There was a rap on the door and a dozen girls, me included, sprinted out to the now empty dance floor. The band started and the girls began to move their hips and kick their legs. I followed along as best as I could, but there was no doubt I was the awkward standout. I imagined our routine was sensational for the time, but it was nothing worse than what anyone could watch on TV any night of the week during family hour at home. It didn't seem to matter. The crowd cheered, guys and girls alike.

Nate was the only one who didn't seem to be having a good time. His eye were hooded and his arms were crossed tightly across his chest as he watched me.

I smiled back at him trying to communicate with my eyes that I was fine and having fun. The easiest ten dollars I'd ever make.

We were just ending what I was soon to learn was the final song when my eyes landed on another face. The man had slicked back hair and thick brows over penetrating eyes. Sheldon Vance. I could tell by the flash of recognition that passed behind his dark eyes that he remembered me. I wondered how he got out of jail. He probably wondered the same about me.

I stumbled with my final leg kick, catching the girl in front of me in the knee and sending her flying. She cried out. Sheldon Vance stepped forward.

It was time to run again.

TWENTY

"Casey Donovan!"

Sheldon shouted my name out in public. I couldn't believe he remembered it! I didn't know what he wanted from me, but I wasn't about to hang around to find out. I pushed through the crowded, hot room and motioned to Nate to head for the door. He saw Sheldon coming after me, and he shoved people aside until he reached me. Looking at me incredulously, he reached for my hand, but didn't say a word. We flung ourselves out the door and up the cement steps to the street and ran.

Jumping around on stage in two-inch heels and a skimpy feather laden outfit was one thing. Dodging main road traffic, racing down shady side streets and through dark back alleys with a crime-boss-type guy from a mob family on said heels was another.

Dogs barked, horns honked, and we kept running. Nate was in front of me now, dragging me by the wrist. I did my best to keep up, but I was seriously worried I was going to sprain my ankle in these stupid shoes! Nate was a super-athlete with athletic legs and healthy lungs. My lungs felt like they were on fire. My heart beat like a bomb counting down, about to go off.

My ears rang with the sound of a gunshot, and I ducked instinctively, tripping on my heels. I cried out with the pain that exploded in my ankle. Nate pulled me behind a garbage bin and urged me to be quiet. I covered my mouth with my hands, biting down the pain, awash with a very real fear.

I was breathing too heavily. Too loudly. I focused on regulating my breath, breathing into my hands to keep from hyperventilating. *In and out.* Sheldon Vance had a gun. *In and out.* He was hunting us. Hunting me! *In and out.* I was so in over my head! *In and out.*

Footsteps!

Nate squeezed my arm, reminding me to stay still. Keep quiet. The footsteps grew nearer. And nearer. *And nearer!*

Nate sprung out into the street and tackled Sheldon Vance, putting all those years of football mojo into practice. It shocked me so much, I sat momentarily frozen in place. I heard the clank of something heavy hit the ground.

The gun.

My eyes had adjusted to the darkness and there was just enough moonlight so that the metal glinted like a beacon. Nate and Sheldon rolled on the ground, away from the gun. I jumped to sprint for it, forgetting my ankle, and I screamed out in pain. I hopped on one leg. Despite the cool of night, sweat dripped down my brow and into my eyes. I kept my gaze focused on the gun, praying that Nate would be all right. I knew he could hold his own in a fight—I'd seen him do it before. And like this time, he had been fighting because of me. I had put him in danger again.

As I reached the gun, I could hear their heavy breathing and grunts and groans. The pistol was old, well, old for me and my time. I aimed it toward Sheldon, but I couldn't tell who was who in the shadowy darkness.

"I have the gun!" I yelled.

The guys were dark silhouettes rolling on the ground. The one on top dropped a punch and the lower guy slumped.

There was stillness, and black fear pinned me to the spot. "Nate?"

"Yeah," he said, breathing heavily. "I'm okay."

The relief that wooshed through me made me weak in the knees.

Nate lifted himself off Sheldon Vance's body. "Let's get out of here."

"Is he...?"

"He's alive. I just don't want to be here when he comes to."

I inhaled sharply at the sight of Nate's face. "You're hurt," I said. Blood ran from a cut above his eye. His bottom lip was split.

Nate rubbed the blood away with his sleeve. "I'm fine." He took the gun from my shaky hands and tossed it into the garbage bin. "Are you all right?" he asked me.

"I twisted my ankle," I said. It hurt to put pressure on it, but at least I could limp along. Nate put his arm under my shoulder, so I could lean on him.

"Are you going to tell me what that was all about?" he said. "Why was that guy after you?"

I fudged. "I'm not sure."

"He knew your name, Casey." He rubbed his forehead and winced like it hurt him to do so. I didn't doubt he had a major headache. "How is that possible?"

I'd told Nate about tripping in Hollywood to explain the time reset, but I hadn't told him *everything*. There hadn't been time, really, and truthfully, I was hoping to avoid it. Nate had this belief that I couldn't trip without getting into some kind of trouble. As if traveling back in time wasn't its own sort of trouble. It would be nice if I could just trip back, live quietly and uneventfully until the time came, mysteriously as always, to shoot me through the light back to my present.

We kept walking, I wasn't sure where to, and I told him about the bank robbery.

"We thought it was a legitimate job! A movie set." Though now, looking back, I could see that a lot had been missing. Like director chairs, and lights, and cameras already inside the bank. I didn't see the need to mention those details.

"My dear girl. They threw ya in the slammeh, did they?" Nate said with the rushed monotone style of speech of the day.

I nudged him with my elbow. "This isn't funny."

His expression dropped. "Believe me, I'm not laughing."

I groaned. Here I was without a proper dress in the cool evening, a bum ankle, a boyfriend whose face was bruised and bleeding, and nowhere to go.

And I didn't even have the ten dollars to show for the trouble.

"So, you helped him rob a bank. You'd think he'd be grateful. Why isn't he?"

I sighed. "All the mob guys wore hose over their heads, making it hard for people who hadn't seen them without the disguise, recognize him. But Sheldon has distinctive eyebrows. He knows I saw him shoot the teller."

"He *shot* someone?" Nate let out an exasperated breath. "Then what happened?"

"Sheldon didn't get away. I saw them drag him into the jailhouse, and he saw me see him. His gangster family must've gotten him off somehow."

"And now he sees you as a threat to upsetting that."

"I guess so."

"You're a witness." It was a statement, not a question, and I couldn't miss the dread in his voice.

I swallowed. "Yes."

We turned a corner onto another street lined with brownstones and stopped as a blond girl exited a taxi and ran up the steps.

"Hey, that's..." Nate started.

I called out, "Marlene!"

She turned with a start and frowned when she recognized us. "*There* you are! Do you know that Barbara wanted to charge me for your costume? Said I brought you in, I should pay."

"I'm so sorry, Marlene," I said. "We had to leave quickly..."

She placed a hand on her narrow hips. "Yeah, I saw."

"Please, do you know of somewhere safe we could go for the night?" I sounded like I was begging, and I was.

Marlene cocked her head and stared at Nate. "You look like you need to get cleaned up. Fine. Come on in."

I leaned on Nate as we climbed the cement steps and I let out a breath of relief when he shut the door of the brownstone behind us.

The foyer opened up to a living area. One thing I was surprised about was how colorful the decor was. I'd only seen black and white photos of the era, and I hadn't pictured it like this. There were two armchairs and a short sofa made of emerald green fabric with gold stitching. A brick fireplace in the middle of the wall had a framed panoramic print of Boston Harbor. Interestingly, a small round table with two ladder-back chairs painted blood-orange red sat in the middle of the room. A large yellow area rug lay on the hardwood floors. A writing desk in the corner was painted sagebrush green. Everything was fresh and new. Marlene's family were enjoying the extravagance of the age.

Marlene motioned for us to sit, then disappeared. Nate sat in on one of the wooden chairs while I plopped onto the sofa and rested my leg on the soft armrest. Marlene reappeared and returned with a chunk of ice wrapped in a towel, a damp cloth and a small first-aid kit. She handed the ice to me, and I winced as I placed the burning cold onto my swollen ankle.

Marlene shifted the second chair close to Nate and began to nurse his face, a task she seemed to enjoy if you could go by her gleeful countenance. "I suppose you could stay here tonight," she finally said. "My mother will be put out, but I can deal with her in the morning. My sister Shirley left for North Carolina so there's an extra bed." She paused to pat her blond bob, and smiled at Nate. "You can take the sofa."

"That would be great," Nate murmured.

Marlene opened a tube filled with some kind of ointment and patted it gently on Nate's face. I cursed my bum foot. *I should be the one up front and personal with Nate, not a pretty blond stranger!*

"You look like you come from a good family," I ventured. "So..."

She cut me a wide-eyed look. "So why am I dancing at an illegal club?"

"Yeah?" I thought it was a fair question.

Marlene turned back to Nate and applied a bandage to the cut above his eye. "To make extra money, which I'm *not* blowing on booze and cigarettes like the other girls." Marlene threw her shoulders back proudly. "I'm investing in stocks. I'm making heavy sugar!"

"Don't do that," Nate said.

I widened my eyes and subtly shook my head, but Nate wasn't looking at me. His gaze was on Marlene.

She grinned back with a flirtatious glint in her eye. "Oh, bunny, why wouldn't I?"

"Because the market's going to crash."

"Nate!" I shouted. Sheldon's punches had knocked the sense right out of him!

His expression flattened like he knew he said too much.

Marlene sat back. "Ah, applesauce. The economy has never been stronger. Everyone has a radio, automatic appliances, and most people can afford a car. Well, except the farmers, but most city folk are doing nifty. In fact—" Her eyes glinted with pride, "—with my stock earnings, I'll be buying an automobile for myself soon, maybe even get my own place."

Time to change the subject and end this terrible day!

"Thanks so much for your help, Marlene," I said. "We don't want to keep you up too late."

Marlene patted Nate on the knee before standing and I rolled my eyes. She left us alone again and Nate and I fell into an awkward silence. She returned with bedding for the couch. I shifted off and she prepared it with precision. She straightened, patted her blond bob *again*, and smiled at Nate *again*. "There, you're sitting pretty!"

I yawned with an exaggerated effort. "Wow, I'm so tired." Must get dance-flirt away from my boyfriend! "Can we..."

Marlene nodded agreeably. "Ya, sure. We're upstairs."

"'Night, Nate," she said with a little wave. Nate waved back, then gave me a sheepish look. I wished Nate would approach me, kiss me goodnight or at least hug me, but he turned to the washroom and disappeared behind the door.

TWENTY-ONE

I FOLLOWED Marlene up the steps and she pointed to the empty bed in her room. "I'd like the dance clothes back, but help yourself to anything in my sister's closet," she said. "There's a nightgown in the dresser."

"Thanks," I said, hoping the irritation I felt didn't seep out into my voice.

She grabbed her nightclothes and walked down the hall to the bathroom. I heard the shower turn on.

Marlene's bedroom was another color sensory blast. Pink walls, green carpet, yellow dressing table. The single beds had metal pipe headboards and footboards and wine-color comforters. Framed black and white photos hung on the wall. One was of Marlene and a girl who looked a lot like her. Must be the sister Shirley. Beside it was one of Marlene laughing with another pretty girl who had a dark bob, big eyes and a bright smile. A best friend, maybe?

I changed into the nightgown, and pulled the pins out of my hair, letting it flow long, down my back.

I climbed into Shirley's bed, was so relieved to be safe and warm in comfortable sheets, I feel asleep immediately.

I AWOKE to the smell of bacon and fried eggs. Voices floated up the stairs. I recognized Nate's but couldn't decipher what he was saying. Marlene's giggle was hard to miss, too.

I scrambled out of bed. Had I slept in? I really didn't like the idea of Nate and Marlene eating breakfast together without me, especially since it smelled like she was also a pretty good cook. I hurried as fast as I could in the washroom, washing the makeup off my face and rinsing my mouth. I didn't know what to do about clothing. I didn't have anything except the granny nightgown I was wearing. Good enough. I headed down the steps, favoring my bum ankle, but thankful that it didn't hurt nearly as bad as it had the night before.

"Good morning," Marlene said when she spotted me. Unlike me, she looked as fresh as a daisy and wore a clean, flattering, flapper-style dress. She sat next to Nate.

I forced a smile. "Good morning." I kept my gaze on Nate as I drew out the chair on the other side, kitty-corner from him. "It smells great."

"Help yourself," Marlene said. She pushed the half-empty dishes toward me. I accepted them and filled my plate.

"Did you sleep well?" she asked.

"Yes, thanks." I glanced at their empty dishes. "Too well, it seems."

I turned to Nate, keeping my expression calm. "How was the sofa?"

"Slept like a baby."

Marlene rested her palm on Nate's arm. "I'm so glad!"

I had long arms, but not quite long enough to swat her hand off my boyfriend's arm. Before I could do anything I would likely regret later, I was startled by a matronly voice.

"So, there *is* a female companion."

A woman I presumed was Marlene's mother stood at the opposite end of the room. Her salt-and-pepper hair formed a large, loose bun on the top of her head. Her long-sleeved blouse was buttoned to the top in a cuff around her neck. Her dark skirt dragged on the floor. She didn't look at all pleased to see me.

"Yes, Mama," Marlene said with a slight roll of her eyes. "I wouldn't invite a single man to spend the night in our house."

Mrs. Charter frowned at me as her eyes scanned me from head to toe. "Have you nothing decent to wear to breakfast?"

"I... Um.. I..."

"Her garments were ruined yesterday by a car driving too fast through a puddle," Marlene said. "I'll lend her something of mine."

Mrs. Charter huffed. "I said something *decent*."

Marlene leaned toward Nate and me and spoke in a faux whisper. "Ma thinks I dress inappropriately."

"I can hear you, Marlene. I may be growing older, but my ears are in fine condition." She pointed a finger. "Young people today have no respect for their elders. They have too much time and money, wear too much makeup and not enough clothing. And don't get me going on those wretched automobiles!"

Marlene's eyes sparkled with amusement. "The modern automobile is an excuse for unchaperoned debauchery."

"Marlene!"

"Sorry, Mama."

Marlene didn't sound sorry. In fact, I thought she enjoyed teasing her mother who obviously had not adjusted to the changing times.

Mrs. Charter spun on her heel and Marlene grinned at Nate. "In fact, I think I'm going shopping for an automobile today."

I choked on a piece of bacon. Did Marlene not understand that Nate and I were together? By the way she was overtly flirting, apparently not. He did nothing to set her straight, just grinned back at her. I kicked his leg under the table.

"Ow. What the heck, Casey."

"Oh, sorry." I faked a look of concern. "Did I hurt you?"

He rubbed his shin. "It's fine."

"Would you like more coffee, Nate?" Marlene asked.

"No, I'm good," Nate said. "I'm nice and full. The breakfast was fantastic."

"I wouldn't mind a cup," I said. Thanks for asking.

"Oh, sure." She lifted the pot and wrinkled her nose. "It's empty. I'll go make another pot."

She left for the kitchen and Nate and I were finally alone.

"I think this is your new family, Casey," he whispered.

Was that why he was being so friendly? To make sure I was "in" with them?

"Maybe," I said. I wasn't ready to commit to anything, but beggars couldn't be choosers and Shirley's bed was warm and comfortable. The whole idea of me having to reprogram my alternate reality to this era and these people made me feel dizzy.

Dizzy!

I gripped Nate's hand as I stood sharply. "We need to go!"

"What? Oh!"

We hurried out the front door and closed it behind us before Marlene could return and witness our disappearance. I was thankful that I always had lead time before tripping back to my present. I held on tightly to Nate's hand. No way did I want to leave him behind with Marlene, not even for a moment!

With a tumble through a flash of light, we were back in the present at the exact same spot at Boston University from where we'd left. I no longer wore Marlene's sister's nightgown and Nate was out of his trousers and back in his jeans.

We were back, but it only took a split second to register that something was very, very wrong.

TWENTY-TWO

THE DORM TOWERS WERE GONE. The campus lights were out. A quick tour confirmed my worst fears. Most of the recognizable buildings in the area had disappeared and there were a few in place that hadn't been there before.

A heavy dark pit spread through my churning gut. "Oh no," I said.

Nate's expression was pure panic. "What happened?" He looked like he was going to collapse in on himself. I'd never see him look so stricken.

"We must've changed the timeline," I whispered. I felt hollow and helpless. What other changes lie beyond the campus grounds?

"But, I thought..." His voice was weak and thin. "It never..."

He was speechless, and I understood why. I'd traveled back in time a myriad of times and no matter what happened, no matter what I did, or even what Nate or Tim had done, the timeline never changed when we got back to our present. Everything was always exactly the same, and no one ever knew anything extraordinary had happened to me. They were sometimes baffled by a sudden change in my hair, pulled up when it had been down, for example, or they might notice dark rings suddenly appearing under my eyes, but that was it.

My theory was that since I'd already lived through the past, whatever I was going to do there, had already been done, so there was no way for me to change the future, because my future was a result of the past I'd already lived through—even if I hadn't done it yet to my knowledge.

It was twisted logic that made my head hurt, but my theory had held tight.

Until now.

"It must be a result of the reset," I said. "I was born to go back to the 1800s. It was my natural loop. This loop to the 1920s wasn't supposed to happen."

Nate ran a hand through his hair. This was the first time I'd ever seen him look so scared and it scared me. He had dark rings under his eyes—I knew I had them too—but they were worse than I'd ever seen them before. He had a black eye and a split lip and he hadn't slept in over twenty-four hours. I worried he was going to crack on me.

"We need to find a place to rest," I said. "We need time to think."

Nate shook his head. "I don't know where. I don't know this place anymore."

"Maybe we should go home," I said. "Back to Cambridge."

He shot me a look. "We don't know what we'll find there either."

Nate was right. If Boston had changed, it stood to reason that Cambridge had as well. I felt heavy with anxiety and fatigue, and on the verge of tears. I needed to lie down and think.

"The old dorm buildings are still here," Nate said. "Let's check them out."

I followed Nate, hoping we'd find students there. Maybe someone could help us by shedding light on what had happened.

My heart sank as we drew closer. The walls were full of graffiti, and the windows were boarded up.

"They're abandoned," I said.

"Let's find a way in," Nate said. "It's shelter at any rate."

I agreed with him. This version of the campus was closed down, but it wasn't empty. There were other people milling about, slowly, like they didn't have a place to go either.

We snuck around the back, until we found a ground-level window that had a board jimmied away. Someone else had done this before us. Maybe they were still inside?

"Nate?"

He sensed my concern. "I'm sure it's just people like us, looking for a place to crash."

I hoped Nate was right. It didn't look like there was anything left to steal, so what other reason would anyone have for being here?

Nate went first and then helped me in, which I appreciated since my ankle was still complaining.

The only light in the room came from the crack between the board and the window. The space was vacant except for a few abandoned desks. Dust covered everything, and I held in a sneeze. I didn't think there would be a comfy bed lying around waiting for us. I had hoped for something other than the industrial-looking carpet on the floor, but at least it was carpeted.

Nate didn't waste any time and dropped to the floor and onto his back. He draped his arms over his chest and closed his eyes, then peeked at me. He patted the ground beside him, and I almost cried with happiness. I snuggled against him for warmth and he did the same. It was so good to be held by Nate again. A little sprout of hope poked out of my heart.

His breathing slowed and deepened to a soft snore. Even though we'd both just had a night of sleep, tripping home always took a physical toll. Sleep didn't come as easily for me. The events of the past day flooded my mind. So much had happened, it felt like weeks of stuff rather than hours. Nate returned from Spain. He saw the picture of me kissing Austin. I trained into Boston to talk to him in person. A third picture of Austin and me was circulated. We got a block away from Nate's dorm before spiraling to 1929. We hid out in a clothing factory and sewed ourselves costumes. We "borrowed" coats and boots from interlopers. We crashed a speakeasy and I danced for hire. Sheldon Vance chased us. Shot at us. Nate wrestled him to the ground and knocked him out. Marlene took us off the street, gave us a place to sleep and fed us breakfast.

And now we were crashing in an abandoned building in a timeline that wasn't our own with no idea what to do next.

I focused on the rhythm of Nate's breath and eventually dozed a little. When my eyes fluttered open again, Nate was standing by a window, peering out through a crack in the boards. I couldn't tell if he was still mad at me or if everything that had happened since yesterday made my stupid kissing mistake inconsequential. Nate had always stood by me. No matter how crazy things had gotten, and they had gotten pretty crazy at times, he'd never faltered.

But this was different. Despite allowing me to lie close to him to keep warm, he didn't offer me comfort or verbal reassurance. The way he looked at me when he turned away from the window... it was like he was angry. Angry and trying very hard not to be. The conflict on his face was difficult to hide, and I didn't blame him. Things were really screwed up this time, and I didn't know how to fix it.

TWENTY-THREE

NATE REACHED into his back pocket and pulled out his wallet. "I'm out of cash," he said, "but I have a bank card."

The bank on campus was out of order, but Nate knew where one was in the next neighborhood and thankfully, it was still standing and functioning.

Unfortunately, Nate's card didn't work. He let out a frustrated sigh.

"Let's go home," I said. "Our parents have to be around, even in this altered timeline, and I'm sure they'll feed us."

"Okay," Nate said.

I had my transit card in my pocket. We could get on the train even if the card didn't work. We'd just have to dodge the ticket reader if we saw one.

The rest of Boston seemed relatively unchanged, though some middle-class areas looked more run down. Whatever we did to cause the alteration effected the university most of all.

We sat side by side on the train, but not touching. Nate

sighed repeatedly and I almost slapped my hand over his mouth. The people on the train looked normal enough, a mix of teens, young moms with kids and nightshift workers on their way home. No aliens or cyborgs. Whatever we did, it didn't change the nature of species occupying planet Earth, though there were a couple of overly pierced green-haired punks sitting across from us who were vying for the position.

Since Nate's house was before mine on our route, we went there first. I almost suggested that I go on to my place on my own, but I didn't know for sure what Nate would find at his house and I didn't want to leave him alone until I knew he'd be okay.

His old '82 BMW sat parked in the spot beside his house and I could sense Nate's relief radiate off him. This was still his house. It looked much the same, except that it could use a coat of paint and the landscaping was less than shipshape. The Mackenzie house had always been the sharpest-looking one on the street with a perfectly trimmed hedge, well pruned trees and brightly coloured flowers. Now it was slightly over grown and the lawn was spotted with dry patches.

Nate removed a key from its hiding place under one of the many planters under the living-room window—another sign that things were on track with Nate's life, at least in Cambridge—and we went inside.

"Mom?" Nate called out. "Dad?"

"In here," his mom said, her voice coming from the direction of the kitchen.

I followed Nate to the kitchen entrance and ran into his back when he stopped suddenly. His mom looked so different from when I last saw her, like she had gained thirty pounds. Instead of stylish clothes and a short salon cut, she wore a frayed housecoat and her hair was up in a greasy bun.

"Where were you all night?" she said with a look of disapproval. Then her eyes settled on me. "Oh, hello."

"Just out," Nate said, recovering from his initial shock. "We're starving."

"You know where the bread is," his mom said as she stirred sugar into a cup of coffee. "Butter and jam is in the fridge. Keep it down. Your father just got in from an overnight flight and he's sleeping."

"Okay, Mom, thanks," Nate said.

"No problem." She stopped and looked at him pointedly. "Are you going to introduce me to your friend?"

Nate's startled gaze darted to mine. We'd been going out together for almost two years. I'd met Mrs. Mackenzie dozens of times.

"This is Casey," Nate finally said.

"Nice to meet you," she said with tight lips. I got the feeling she didn't approve of Nate staying out all night with strange girls. A sentiment I shared actually.

Mrs. Mackenzie tightened the belt of her housecoat and patted her hair like she'd suddenly become self-conscious with me in the room. She cast another look of disapproval before leaving Nate and me alone in the kitchen.

Nate slipped two pieces of bread into the toaster and poured two glasses of apple juice. I was parched and gulped my glass down. Nate refilled it.

"The fridge is pretty barren," he said quietly. "And my mom... I don't think she's selling real estate anymore."

The toast popped and I buttered it while Nate toasted two more pieces.

"I should go home," I said, after finishing my plate of toast. "Thanks for breakfast. I'll text you if I still have a phone."

"I don't think I have a phone anymore," Nate said. "At any rate, I'm not letting you go home alone."

"I'll be fine," I said, though I didn't really believe it. I just didn't want Nate to do anything else out of obligation to me.

Nate just shook his head and made for the front door. He glanced back at me. "Coming?"

His keys to his BMW hung on a hook by the entrance, and he grabbed them on the way out. It was a long walk to my place from his and a cumbersome bus route. I appreciated the ride.

"Are we going to be okay?" I asked softly after we'd ridden in silence for a few minutes.

"We'll figure something out," Nate said, misunderstanding my question.

I reached for his hand. "I mean, are *we* going to be okay?"

He pulled his hand away to shift gears, and kept his eyes on the road. He hesitated a little too long before saying, "Sure."

I swallowed the lump in my throat, more worried now than ever that I was losing him. But even if Nate wanted to break up, he couldn't get rid of me yet. If we were going to fix this—and I had no idea how we were going to do that—we needed each other.

He turned on my road but didn't bother pulling into my drive. Because it didn't exist. He pulled up in front of the house where mine normally sat. I double-checked the address. The house looked completely different. My house was a standard colonial with a flat front, symmetrical windows framed with black wooden shutters. This one was modern contemporary.

That didn't mean I didn't live here. I ran to the front door and pulled on the handle, but it was locked. I knocked on the door, fully expecting to stare down at my worried mother's face, or maybe my father's angry one, or maybe my brother's annoyed one, but a strange woman with dark hair and brown skin opened the door.

"Can I help you?" the lady asked.

"I'm looking for the Donovan family," I said with a tremor in my voice. "They... used to live here."

"I don't know that name," she said. "If they lived here in the past, I wouldn't know." She shrugged. "I'm sorry."

I turned back to Nate in a stupor.

I didn't know where my family was, and I had no idea how to find them.

TWENTY-FOUR

I FELT like a zombie walking back to Nate's car. I folded into the passenger seat and mumbled, "This isn't my house. I don't know where my family is."

Nate gave me a sympathetic look. He reached for my hand and squeezed, a gesture I deeply appreciated. "We'll find them."

I breathed deeply and shuddered. "How?"

"Phone book?" Nate shifted into gear and headed down the road.

"Where are we going?"

"The library."

I couldn't stop staring and blinking in disbelief. Much of the neighborhood looked the same, but then there would be a row of houses designed in an alternate style, like my own house had been, or a missing strip mall. In my world, the library was built in 1888, and it looked a lot like a fairy-tale castle. It was made of pale stone with dark contrasting arches over the main doors. Sloped red ceilings were dotted with gable windows. A turret tower topped with a red cone pointed to the sky. A modern boxy, rectangular expansion sided with a glass curtain and three times the size of the original library had opened in 2011.

The new expansion was missing.

I gulped.

Nate's jaw went slack. "I hope they still have computers.

"You need a library card to use the computers," I said.

Nate removed his wallet and pulled out his card. "I'm hoping, since I have the same street address, that this will still work."

I opened the car door. "You don't need a library card to look at phone books."

The interior of the old library had concave ceilings and a lot of dark wood, reminding me more of an old tavern than a library. The books and tables were laid out differently than I remembered and it took a moment to find the librarian's station. She pointed us to the reference section where we would find the phone books.

The current edition was on top, and I hurriedly searched for my surname along with my parents' names. I ran my finger down the list of Donovans. My heart thudded. There it was: Donovan, Richard and Eloise.

I knew the neighborhood where the address was listed. It was in a low-income area with lots of multi-family housing. "We're living in an apartment?"

I borrowed a pen and scribbled the address on the inside of my arm. Nate took the pen and wrote the phone number on his hand.

"Let's go," Nate said.

It took fifteen minutes to get to the building where I

apparently now lived. It wasn't old in a cool, classic way. It was just old. We rode the elevator to the third floor. It smelled funny, like old sweat and last week's dinners. I found the suite number, 307, and lifted my hand to knock.

Nate grabbed my arm just in time. "You don't knock on the door of your own house."

He was right, but it felt strange to turn the handle and walk in. It was small, with a combined living room/kitchen area, but decorated well, like a home-living magazine, all color-coordinated and tidy. At least my mom still had her flare for design. I called out, "Mom?"

"Casey?" Mom walked out of one of the rooms off the hallway. She looked the same with honey-blond hair tucked behind her ears. She wore jeans and a crisp button-up blouse. "You're back from the library already? I thought you just left?"

She stopped when her eyes landed on Nate. "Oh. Hi." She held out a hand. "I'm Eloise."

Nate's eyes darted to me briefly before he accepted her hand. "Nate Mackenzie. A friend of Casey's."

"Do you go to the same school?"

"No, he's in university," I said quickly.

"Really," Mom mused. "Which one?"

Oh, man. Boston U isn't functioning. Should I say Harvard, or MIT? She'd wonder how we met and why he was with me.

"Actually, I'm just applying for next semester," Nate said. "Not sure which one I'll be in."

"You're working?"

Mom! Why so many questions? Time to deflect.

"Is Tim here?"

Mom frowned. "Was he supposed to come today?"

What did she mean, supposed to come? Didn't he live here?

"Where else would he be?"

"Your dad didn't say."

I cast an anxious glance at Nate. He shrugged subtly and said, "I have to go." Behind my mom's head, he made the universal "I'll call you sign," and pointed to the number on his hand.

"Okay," I said. "Thanks for the ride."

I excused myself before Mom could grill me. I needed time to get my story straight. Mom stayed behind in the kitchen, and I hunted for the bathroom. Thankfully, all the doors in the hall were open and I found what I was looking for. The bathroom was decorated in soft, marine blues with shades of purple and pink. Fairly feminine. My pulse accelerated as I opened the doors of the cabinets, looking for signs of a masculine presence. Not one bottle of shaving cream or aftershave to be found. This was not good!

I continued down the hall and found a storage room and two bedrooms, Mom's and mine. Hers had a desk under the window where she managed her work, and I assumed she was still in interior design. I skipped lightly to the closet, and my chest tightened at the continued evidence. No men's clothing hung on the rod.

The apartment had no sign of Tim at all, outside of a few photos of us as kids hanging on the wall.

It was clear that my parents were separated and Tim lived with my dad. There wasn't much I could do now but investigate my own belongings. Most of the objects were duplicates of what I had in my own timeline. I wore the same kinds of clothes. There were a few small differences, like all the photos of Lucinda and me were missing. There was a cell phone on the dresser, mine. I searched for her number, but she wasn't listed in my contacts. Strange.

There was a laptop on my bed. I opened it up and did a white pages search. I called Lucinda's home number.

"Hi. This is Casey Donavan. Is Lucinda there?"

"Hold on one minute."

I waited and my nerves tingled. Finally, Lucinda answered. "Hello?"

"Hey, Luce, it's me. The craziest thing happened and I don't have your cell phone number anymore."

"Who's this?"

Blood whooshed through my ears. Lucinda knew my voice. "It's Casey."

"Casey?"

My throat felt tight as I forced out my last name. "Donovan."

"Casey Donovan? Why are you calling me?"

"Because we're friends?"

She confirmed what I already feared by saying, "That's news to me."

"Oh." I swallowed the lump that had formed in my throat. "Okay, well, sorry to have bothered you."

I crawled onto my bed and curled up into a ball. Everything was such a big huge mess! My parents were divorced, I had no idea what kind of relationship I had with my brother, and my best friend sounded like she detested me. On top of that, Nate was as cold as a cucumber toward me. A single tear escaped out of the corner of my eye, down my cheek and onto my pillow.

TWENTY-FIVE

ANOTHER WHITE PAGES search produced the California number I was looking for. She answered on the fourth ring.

"Hello?"

"Adeline?"

"Yeah?"

"It's Casey Donovan from Cambridge. Do you remember me?"

"My memory's not that bad." I could hear the humor in her voice. "I think I can recall the last few days."

"Oh, thank God!" I almost cried with relief.

She paused then asked, "Is something wrong?"

I pinched the bridge of my nose and tried to steady my breath. "Yes, terribly wrong. Is there anything wrong on your end?"

"Everything seems fine." Her voice was all seriousness now. "Casey, what happened? You're making me nervous!"

"I tripped with Nate, but we didn't go back to my loop of 1883."

"You're stuck in 1929, then? Was it hard to navigate?"

"Kind of, but that's not the problem." I paced the narrow area beside my bed, where the blue rug had worn out to a dirty gray. "The problem is, we got back to the present, but everything's changed."

"How so?"

"Boston University is shut down, my parents are split up, and I live with my mom in an old apartment building. My best friend and I aren't friends. It just goes on, Adeline. It's like we caused a local economic collapse."

"Oh, Casey."

"You're sure nothing has changed in California?"

"Not that I can tell."

"I hope the changes we caused are restricted to this area, then. Still..."

Adeline finished for me. "It's bad news. I haven't travelled back to 1929 since you left. Does this mean I could change the order of things if I do?"

Oh, man! Does this mean we might keep changing the timeline now, every single time we travel? That would be catastrophic. Nate and I had been gone only one day and look at the damage we'd done!

"You have to be really careful," I said. "Try to hole up somewhere and stay out of trouble."

"I'm guessing *you* didn't stay out of trouble."

"Not exactly. Sheldon Vance was there."

"He's out of prison?"

"Yes. And he saw me. Nate and I had to run."

"He chased you? Why did he do that?"

"Well, I obviously wasn't in jail in California. He

managed to get released and maybe he thought I was a threat to him getting thrown back in?"

"Oh, Casey! So what happened next?"

"He and Nate got into a scuffle." I decided to leave out the part about the gun. No need to freak her out more than I already had.

"Do you think meeting up with Sheldon again caused your timeline to change?"

"It's possible, I guess." I groaned loudly. "Oh, this is such a mess. And on an even more personal note, Nate is freezing me out."

"Ah, you told him about the kiss."

"I didn't have a chance. Someone's been posting pictures!"

"Pictures? As in more than one?"

"Three so far."

"Yikes. Sounds like someone's after your man."

"And he's angry about my new loop, not to mention the fact that he's no longer at BU."

"That's a lot of stuff, Casey. I'm really sorry about you and Nate, but as hard as it is, it's your second-priority problem. You need to get back to 1929 and undo whatever it is you did and hope you can straighten things out. Just because I can't see any obvious changes around me, doesn't mean there aren't any. I haven't been following the news lately."

"I know. I'll have to try to trigger a trip back somehow. Nate's coming to get me soon. We'll figure it out."

"Keep me posted."

"Will do!" Since Adeline was officially the only friend I currently had on the planet, it was a promise I knew I would keep.

. . .

NATE CALLED me later that night as promised.

"Apparently, I don't go to university anywhere." He sounded disgusted. "I work at a car parts shop."

"Yeah, well, Lucinda and I aren't even friends. I have no idea who my friends are here. Mom expects me to go to school tomorrow, but I'm certain that will be a disaster."

"We should go back to the library again," Nate said. "We need to find out what happened to change everything. Then we need to go back and fix this."

"I agree," I said, "but I don't think you should come to the door. Mom seemed overly suspicious of you."

Nate chuckled. "I'm an older guy with no prospects. She has reason to be wary."

I wanted to laugh, but I couldn't muster it. "I'll meet you at the corner by the deli," I said. "Seven-thirty."

Eating breakfast with Mom the next morning was a little awkward. There was so much I was supposed to know that I didn't. I needed to dig for answers without making her think I fell on my head or something.

I went through a couple cupboards before finding the cereal, a bowl and a spoon. At least the milk was easy to locate in the fridge.

"Ah, when is Tim coming to see us?" I asked. Mom's eyes peeked out from behind her coffee mug. "Next weekend. I thought you were going to a concert together."

"Oh, yeah, right."

There was a newspaper opened to Mom's right and she was circling ads.

"Are you looking to buy something?" I asked.

She huffed. "No money to buy stuff, Casey. You know that. I'm looking for job leads."

"But...don't you want to work from home?"

She cut me a look like I wasn't making sense. This was harder than I thought it'd be.

"Bretton Wiles wants me in the office where he can breathe over my shoulder. I can't leave Bretton Wiles Interiors until I find something new." She sighed. "The economy is so bad, I should just be thankful I have anything at all. "

"What's wrong with Bretton Wiles?"

"He's an idiot. Casey, you're acting like you haven't heard the stories. Working for Wiles is a nightmare." Mom checked the time and nodded to me. "You better get going. You're going to be late for school."

I'd showered earlier and put on fresh clothes. All I had to do was brush my teeth and add a little makeup.

I guess I didn't need to do that last part. Nate had seen me without makeup tons of times, but I wanted to look my best, or at least a close second. Nate had cooled toward me by several degrees. It made my heart sting, and I wasn't sure, when this was all over, if we'd survive as a couple. I hoped so. I really, really hoped so.

My stomach squeezed a little when I saw him sitting in his old BMW at the curb on the corner.

"Hey," I said as I got in.

"Hey."

I leaned in slightly, hoping he'd meet me halfway for a kiss, but he just signaled and turned onto the road. I sighed and did up my seatbelt.

"How was your night?" I asked, trying to keep my voice light.

"Interesting. My brother John is dead, killed in Iraq. My mother is a borderline alcoholic and my dad is a jerk."

"Oh, Nate. I'm so sorry. We'll figure out a way to fix this."

"I sure hope so."

"What did we do in 1929 that could've triggered these changes?" I said. "And why are some things affected and not others? Why Boston U and not Harvard? Why do I live in an apartment while your family remains in the same house?"

"All good questions."

"Was it Sheldon Vance?" I asked. My voice dropped a tone. "He *was* still alive when we left him, wasn't he?"

"Yes, he was."

"How can we be sure he didn't die in the street?"

"I didn't hit him that hard, Casey. He wasn't bleeding from the back of the head or anything. Just a blow to the jaw."

"Then it had to be Marlene. Maybe she followed your advice and sold her stocks before the crash?"

Nate shook his head. "Even if she did, why would that change so many things? How could that result in the closing down of BU?"

I shrugged. "I don't know. It does seem like a big leap."

Nate used his library card to get access to the computers. We had to wait in line since there were only two. We could've used our own, but we didn't want to spend the time at each other's places with our moms around, and we didn't have any money to spend at a coffee shop. It would be easier to concentrate in the quiet of the library anyway.

Once the guy in front of us finally left, Nate signed on and immediately began looking up the Vance brothers and Sheldon Vance in particular. "Sheldon Vance was the second son of the notorious Vance brothers, a crime family who ran liquor runs during prohibition. He died along with his brother Spenser in a bank robbery gone wrong in 1931."

"So, he did survive our encounter," I said. "Check Marlene Charter."

Nate entered her name in the search.

"Marlene Esposito, Nee, Charter - made her fortune in the stock market in the twenties as a young woman while working as a dancer in the speakeasies of Boston during the prohibition era. When most people were buying stock in large quantities, she inexplicably sold her shares at the end of September, one month before the crash that turned hundreds of millionaires into paupers overnight."

Nate shot me a nervous glance. "She went on to invest in several successful businesses, and while many of those prospered, her involvement on the board of directors of Boston University..." Nate's green eyes cut to me before continuing to read, "caused immense controversy."

I leaned in to peer over his shoulder. "What kind of controversy?"

"Looks like it has something to do with the 2008 Wall Street crash. Her grandson, William Bledoe was the CEO of Grand Central Bank and encouraged the unscrupulous lending of mortgages to people who were under-qualified. She pressured the board of BU to re-mortgage the university property and expand beyond their financial capabilities. When Wall Street crashed, the university had to forfeit its loans. It was the only university in America to go bankrupt in the history of American universities."

"I wonder if my parents got into a bad mortgage? Maybe that's why we don't live in a house anymore." And why my parents gave up on their marriage.

Nate looked at me with remorse. "I should've kept my big mouth shut."

"You couldn't have known. You just wanted to help one girl who was helping us."

"Instead, I created a monster." He dragged his hands through his hair. "The question is what do we do now?"

"We have to find a way back. Convince her to leave her money in stocks," I said.

Nate frowned. "She'll go bankrupt. What will happen to her then?"

"Whatever was supposed to happen," I snapped. I hated how he sounded *concerned* about her. I softened my tone. "She's obviously a resourceful girl. I'm sure she'll figure something out."

Nate sat back and studied me. "The question is, how do we get back?"

I bit my lip as I considered this. Stress was my trigger. Making out with Nate use to be enough to send me back in time, but that stopped happening a while ago, which ultimately was a good thing. It once happened with impromptu public speaking, but I seemed to adapt to certain stressful situations. What worked once, doesn't always work twice. Sometimes stress needs to build, like a long boil, and sometimes it can flick the switch quickly.

"I don't know."

Nate rubbed his forehead like he was trying to erase the lines that had formed there. "We have to do something together." His eyes locked with mine. "We have to go back together."

"I totally agree!" Nate was referencing a time when I pulled my hand away so that I'd trip without him, and that turned into a big disaster. I wasn't about to pull that stunt again. "But what?" I added.

"Something where our feet remain firmly on the ground," he said.

I nodded. No bungee jumping or roller coaster rides. That could be tragic.

"Some kind of pseudo stress," he continued. "Where you feel like you're endangered, but you're really not."

"Play chicken?"

Nate shook his head sharply. "Too dangerous."

"But, it could work. We jump onto the tracks and hop off just before the train reaches us."

"Casey! Do you have a death wish?"

"You said endangered!"

"But not *real* danger. Besides, if it didn't work, we'd get arrested, then what?"

I folded my arms frustrated at being shot down. "It's just an idea. Do you have a better one?"

"We could jump off a building."

"Now who has a death wish?"

"Just a couple floors, into a garbage bin full of something soft."

"Like fabric?"

"Yeah, like fabric."

Nate did a search for textile factories in the area and came up with a name and address. Not the one in Boston, which was now an empty closed-down building that had been a trendy coffee shop in our old timeline, but one on the outskirts of Cambridge. I'd found some cash in my bedroom earlier, so catching a bus wasn't an issue. We left the library and caught the next bus.

We hopped off a block and a half away from the two-story factory warehouse. Metal steps zigzagged from the roof to the ground as a fire escape. The signage was undersized since it wasn't a retail outlet, though there was a small discount store on the ground level. There was an employee parking lot at the back, and a number of industrial-sized trash containers, big enough that they required a truck to lift and dump them. Fortunately, for us, the bins were full.

"Help me push one to the building," Nate said. He unlocked the wheels beneath it and we rolled it up to the side of the warehouse. I helped to lock the wheels back into place and brushed the dirt off my hands. We moved quickly to the fire escape. We didn't want to get caught—the sooner we jumped, the better.

Nate glanced my way. "You ready for this?"

As ready as I'll ever be. "Uh-huh."

He motioned for me to go first. I grabbed the first rung and heaved myself up. Three minutes later, Nate and I were on the roof.

Two stories might not sound like much, but when you're standing on the roof staring down, it was enough to get the vertigo started. My knees trembled.

We saw movement in the alley. A large man in overalls waved an arm. "Hey! What are you doing up there?"

Nate took my hand and gave me an encouraging nod. "Let's do this."

TWENTY-SIX

I CLOSED my eyes and we jumped. I couldn't stop myself from screaming a little. We hit our target and tumbled about awkwardly in the mess of fabric and foam. Something poked me sharply, and I wondered if I'd just been jabbed with a sewing needle.

Nate's voice broke through the pulsing in my ears. "Are you okay?"

"Did it work?" I'd been dizzy, but I didn't notice the light. Could've been because I had my eyes closed, and I was too busy yelling.

"I can't tell from here," Nate said.

Nate hoisted himself out of the bin and then reached in to help me out. The building looked the same. The cars in the parking lot were contemporary models. I swallowed down my disappointment. "It didn't work."

The maintenance man in orange overalls drew closer and he shouted, "Hey, you punks!" His stout body broke into a jog.

We out ran him easily, jumped into Nate's car and skidded away. Nate glanced at me with fear in his eyes. "Don't you dare trip now!"

I held my heart and took calming breaths. "I'm fine," I said. "Not going anywhere."

Nate tapped his fingers on the steering wheel. "We need a new plan."

"Maybe we need to take a night to think about it," I said. I checked the time on the dashboard. It was almost four o'clock. "I better get back. Mom gets home from work soon, and if I'm not there, she's going to ask questions."

Nate sighed, then I sighed. This was all just one big freaky mess, and I couldn't even remember the last time Nate kissed me.

He pulled up to the curb in front of my building. "Are we all right?" I asked. "I mean, it feels like we've broken up or something."

Nate let his chin fall. "Oh, Casey. Let's just sort this out first, okay? Then we'll deal with the other stuff."

His words were a heavy blow to my heart. He'd just put us on an official hiatus. There was nothing I could do but accept his decision. I smiled weakly and said good-bye.

Mom was already home, which surprised me. But then again, it wasn't like I actually knew her schedule. She stood by the living room window, the one that looked down on the street. She had one arm crossed over her chest and the other hand tugged at a tuft of hair by her ear.

"Who was that?" she asked.

"Uh, Nate. He was here with me yesterday."

Her brows furrowed. "Are you dating?"

I hesitated, then said, "Yeah." I hoped it was still true.

"Since when?"

"Since... a while."

"Don't you think you should've talked to me about this first? He's too old for you."

I dropped my pack onto a kitchen chair and removed my jacket. "He's only two years older."

"That's a lot when you're still in high school."

I stuck out my chin. "I'm graduating soon."

Mom huffed in defeat. "Fine. But bring him home for dinner tomorrow. I want to meet him."

"You did meet him."

She gave me a stern look. "You know what I mean. I'd like to get to know him."

"You mean you'd like to interrogate him."

She shrugged. "You say tomehto, I say tomahto."

"Funny."

I didn't have any idea how to get back to 1929, but I did have an idea on how to make it easier on us when we did got back there. I did an online search for costume shops and was pleased to find one nearby that stayed open until six.

I recovered my banking card on a previous search and used it to check my balance on line. Fortunately, I used the same password in this timeline as in my own. My balance was pretty dismal though, a lot lower than what I was used to, but enough to do what I needed.

"I need to go out for a bit, Mom," I called.

"It's almost supper," she called back.

"I won't be long." I took off before she could respond and force me to stay home.

It took me about ten minutes of speed walking to get to the shop. I was heated up and out of breath when I entered.

To save time, I went directly to the clerk and asked for late 1920s costumes.

She pointed out the section, and I was happy to see I had a few choices. I picked out two flapper dresses, one green and one yellow, both shapeless with low waistbands. I tried on a snug black hat with a droopy rim, a fur shawl (hopefully faux fur!) with floppy fox-tail ends, and a pair of black shoes —clunky two-inch heels with a strap on top of the foot. I grabbed a pair of thick tights and a long strand of pearls. I also picked out some clothes for Nate.

I was a little shocked at the price when the clerk rang it up, and I had just barely enough. I stuffed the clothes into the empty pack I'd brought along.

I hurried home and got back just as Mom called for me to set the table. It was strange to eat dinner with just the two of us.

"Why doesn't Tim live here?" I asked as I scraped the last of my pasta from my plate.

Mom's eyes shifted to mine. "You were there, Casey. The judge let him choose. He chose Dad."

The bitterness in her voice was barely perceptible, but I caught the edge. I pinched my lips together to keep from saying anything else. I'd have to satisfy my curiosity some other way.

I went to bed early, telling Mom I had a lot of homework, which was probably true. I was surprised the school hadn't called. Maybe they didn't do that in this timeline, or maybe not for seniors, or maybe luck was on my side and Mom just missed it. Maybe we didn't have an answering machine. I was dead-tired and wasted no time getting ready for bed. I longed for my pillow and comfy blankets. I fell asleep to the drone of the television show Mom was watching on the other side of the wall.

In what felt like just minutes later, I startled awake by a loud, high-pitched siren. The air smelled weird. Smokey.

"Casey!" My mom rushed in and flicked on the lights. "Quick. There's a fire in the building. We have to get out right now."

My heart rate went from zero to sixty in a second. Mom wouldn't give me time to change, so I just grabbed my backpack and a jacket and slipped on my sneakers.

The halls were filled with tenants filing out in their pajamas. I wore a thin tank top and fleece PJ shorts. I worked my arms into my jacket sleeves as I went down. We were hit with a blast of cool, midnight air as we neared the exit. A firefighter stood outside, holding the door open.

"Quickly, but no running!" he shouted. "Cross the street for instructions."

Mom and I hurried across the road where another firefighter corralled us down a block to a makeshift station where we were told to sign our names on a clipboard. "So we know everyone is out," a police officer explained.

Hot orange flames flickered out of the windows on the fourth floor, just above our apartment. The roof buckled, and a loud collective gasp filled the air as the roof collapsed on one corner.

If we hadn't gotten out when we did, we would've been killed.

I felt dizzy. I let go of my mom's arm and let myself fall into the light.

TWENTY-SEVEN

TRAVELING through time was disorienting enough when you knew where you were going and what to expect. I knew my way around 1863 Cambridge. I had a stash of supplies hidden where no one else would find them. I had a surrogate family and friends.

A lump thickened in my throat as I took in my surroundings. Dawn was just breaking, but already there were people milling about and slow-moving, noisy jalopies on the street. I had to get out of sight before I made a spectacle of myself, standing in an empty lot wearing skimpy pajama's with my long, wildly curly hair hanging down my back. There was a chill in the morning breeze, and my arms and legs broke out in goose bumps.

I thought I'd have Nate along with me to navigate, but I was on my own, and I had to buck up and take care of matters myself. At least I had my backpack with the costumes. I slipped behind an old, wooden building that leaned slightly like it could no longer fight back against the wind. I opened my pack and removed the green dress. I slipped it on over my pajamas, happy that the hem fell to my knees, covering my shorts. The thick pantyhose helped to warm my bare legs. Tying my hair into a low bun, I pulled the hat over top, then I exchanged my sneakers for the two-inch heels. Lastly, I wrapped the faux-fur shawl around my shoulders. I suspected I was over dressed for the time of day. Furs likely didn't come out until evening, but what did I know? Besides, I was cold.

I looked around for a place to hide my backpack, an item that was clearly not from this decade. I considered the building I'd first encountered, but couldn't risk the owner coming to tear it down some day. Development progressed rapidly in the twenties, unlike the nineteenth century, when I could confidently bury supplies without a worry that someone might build a house over top of them or dig them up with a backhoe.

I settled on a groundhog hole, using a stick to make it larger. I took a drink from the bottle of water I'd packed, returned it to the backpack, and then I pushed the whole thing inside the hole and covered it with dirt. I made sure to mark it with sticks and rocks so I could find it again, but not so obvious to attract attention from anyone else who might cut through this lot.

Now I had to find a way into Boston and back to Marlene's brownstone. It was a long walk, and I didn't have any money for a tram, though I supposed I could hitch the bumper again, but I wasn't sure where the rail was. I made my way to a main road, wondering if people hitchhiked in this decade. Men probably did, but I doubted women did. Not the respectable ones anyway.

I had no choice. I walked backward, so I could see the drivers. I avoided men-only occupied vehicles, sticking my thumb out if I saw a woman in the passenger seat. A male driver spotted me and began to slow. I experienced a moment of relief until the woman in the passenger seat flashed me a sour look and poked her husband in the arm. Her voice carried through the opened window. "Keep going, Donald!"

I was beginning to think I would have to walk the whole way when a Model T with a female driver puttered to the curb. None of the vehicles until now had a female driver, so I was surprised and thrilled to see her. She was young, with wide, blue eyes, and more makeup than I was used to seeing on women at this time of day. Her hair was a common brown, but styled with perfect waves that ended at the collar of her dress.

She beckoned me over. "Need a ride?"

"Yes!" I said as I pulled on the door handle. "Thank you!"

"My name's Lolly," she said with a confidence I admired.

"I'm Casey." My hand automatically reached for a seatbelt, but of course there wasn't one. I rested my hands on my lap.

"Where ya headed, Casey?" Lolly asked. She stepped on the clutch with her left foot and put the car into gear.

"North Boston."

"That's where I'm headin'!"

The jalopy jerked as she pulled into traffic. "That's great," I said.

Lolly handled the standard transmission like a pro, hands firmly gripping the large steering wheel at two and ten.

"How long have you been driving?" I asked. She didn't look like she could be much older than I was.

"My pa had me driving the tractor on the farm since I was ten." She spoke loudly as the car roared ferociously. Mufflers weren't well developed yet. "Transitioning to an automobile was a breeze."

Lolly wore a fashionable dress, noticeably better in quality than mine, and I suddenly felt like a chump sitting next to her. She cast casual glances at me, and I could see the question marks in her eyes.

"Where ya from?" she asked. I knew this question would arise eventually so I'd spent my time walking creating a backstory.

"I'm from Cambridge. Grew up on a farm, too." I counted Watson's farm as my time growing up, so up until now, I was telling the truth. I inhaled before diving into the "story" part.

"I'm tired of working on the farm and told my parents I had to leave. Find my own way. I'm heading into the city to look for work."

"And how! Women don't need to be stuck in the kitchen any more. We are *modern* women." She laughed and gave me a *girl-power* look. "I'm going to get a job as a secretary! As soon as I make enough money, I'm movin' into the city, even though it'll break my poor mama's heart."

"Why will it break her heart?"

"I'm the baby of the family, and she doesn't like the idea of me leaving the farm. Plus, she hates the way I dress, and the friends I keep. She hates that I'll have a *job*. But I have to be free, Casey. Be my own woman!"

I smiled with understanding.

"Ma and Pa want me to marry Johnny," Lolly continued, "the farm boy next door, so we could join our farms, but I'm done with farmin' I tell ya." She slapped the steering wheel. "Done."

We came to one of the few traffic lights and Lolly jerked the jalopy to a stop. "Hey, did you hear about that Chicago massacre? Wasn't that somethin'? People just can't stop talkin' about it."

I hadn't had time to brush up on my twentieth-century history but I had a vague idea. "Al Capone?" I said, testing.

"Well, he was in Florida when those seven fellas were lined up against the wall and killed, but the rumor is he was behind it." The light changed back to green, and we puttered forward.

"I bet he never gets arrested." She flashed me a serious look. "I bet he gets away with *murder*."

Talking about Al Capone reminded me of his great-grand-nephew Sam Capone. Al was a bad dude, but that didn't mean his unscrupulous ways were passed down through the genes, did it? My nervousness over Lucinda's new relationship just upped a notch.

We were nearing the Longfellow Bridge. I stared at the 1929 version. It looked much the same, with the "salt and pepper" towers midway, but in much better shape. The sun glistened off the surface of Charles River with a beauty that made me gasp. I loved Boston, no matter the era.

Lolly suddenly remembered why I was hitching a ride into town. "What kind of work ya interested in, Casey?"

"I don't know yet. I have a friend I hope can help me."

"Yeah? What's her name? Maybe I know her."

I hesitated. "Marlene Charter?" I didn't know if Marlene

would consider me a friend, especially now that Nate and I had disappeared without one word of thanks for her hospitality.

"Marlene Charter! Nifty! We're chums! In fact, that's where I'm going right now!"

I gaped at her. "Seriously?"

She frowned a little in confusion. "Why would I lie?"

"No," I said quickly. "I didn't mean I thought you were lying. I just meant, wow, what a coincidence."

She reached over and patted my arm. "It's serendipity, Casey. Serendipity."

I did a little happy dance in my seat. Things had a way of working out. I'd see Marlene today, talk her into leaving her stocks alone, and all would be fine once again. Easy peasy.

I should know better.

TWENTY-EIGHT

"Marlene and I go back to grade school," Lolly said. "Her family used to live on a farm down the road from ours. They sold it when her dad got sick, and they moved into town."

"Did her dad pass away?" I asked.

"Yeah. Years ago." Her eyes darted toward me before cutting back to the road. She geared down as the traffic slowed at the other end of the bridge. "She never told ya?"

"We don't actually know each other that well," I admitted.

Lolly scrutinized me from under her thick eyelashes. "How *do* you know her?"

Ack, the question I wanted to avoid! I didn't know how secret Marlene's dancing gig was. Speakeasy clubs were illegal. She could go to jail if she were discovered. I didn't want to blow the whistle on her. "Ah, we met—"

Just then the car jolted to a stop and Lolly laid on the horn. My body flung forward. Because I didn't have a seatbelt, my right shoulder hit the dash. Thankfully, we hadn't been going that fast but I could tell by the throbbing under my flesh that I'd have a nice bruise. I peered out the window. We were inches away from nailing the big, narrow-rim spare tire attached to the back of the fancy car in front of us. The man driving the car studied us through his oversized rearview mirror. I couldn't miss his full, dark eyebrows furrowed over angry eyes. My blood swooshed through my body as recognition dawned.

Sheldon Vance!

I ducked low.

"Are you all right?" Lolly asked. "Sorry about that sudden stop, but we're fine now. You can sit up."

Except that I couldn't risk that Sheldon would recognize me. "I'm fine. Just hurt my shoulder a little. I stayed bent over, facing away from the window, and rubbed my arm with exaggeration.

The traffic moved slowly and eventually we turned off the main road and out from behind Sheldon Vance's car. I sat up and let out a breath of relief.

"Feeling better?" Lolly asked, concern etched on her face.

"Yeah, I'm fine. Just had to rub it out, you know?"

Lolly pulled to a gentler stop along the curb on a street lined with brownstone row houses. I barely recognized Marlene's place—it looked different in the daylight. The bricks were a lighter shade of red than I'd remembered and the curtains in the window looked more green than blue.

Lolly skipped up the cement steps to the front door and knocked. I followed with far less enthusiasm. I was winging it here. A lump of dread settled in my gut. I was here to fix things, but I could just as easily make things worse.

Marlene opened the door and squealed, delighted at the sight of her long-time friend Lolly. They hugged and laughed.

"Your dress is the berries!" Lolly exclaimed.

Marlene did an impromptu twirl. "I just bought it last week." She eyed Lolly's hair. "Your finger curls are the bees knees!"

Lolly patted them in appreciation. "Thanks!"

Marlene finally took a moment to appraise me. Her friendly demeanor disappeared. "You?"

"Hi," I said, and waved sheepishly. Marlene's gaze ran up and down over my costume. No words of praise for my dress or my hair.

"What are you doing here?"

Lolly's eyes flickered with confusion. "I thought you were friends?"

"That's a stretch," Marlene said. "Where's your boyfriend?"

Figured she'd be more interested in Nate than me. I couldn't blame her. "He had to go. Look, I'm sorry about leaving suddenly after breakfast the other day. It was rude."

"I'd say it was rude. And after my being so helpful and generous."

"Hey," Lolly interjected. "What's going on?"

My mind raced for something to say. Marlene looked like she was about to kick me out, and I couldn't leave before I had somehow convinced her to leave her money in stocks. "I have an explanation," I said quickly. "Nate felt sick and needed fresh air. I took him outside for a bit and he complained about being dizzy. I was worried he had a concussion."

"He seemed fine to me."

"Well, sometime symptoms can be delayed." For emphasis I added, "You should see his shiner!"

"Shiner?" Lolly asked.

Marlene's expression mellowed. "Is he okay?"

I nodded. "He's resting at home."

Lolly crossed her arms and tapped her foot. Marlene threaded her arm through Lolly's. "Don't worry. Everything's Jake. Casey's sheik got into a street fight. I helped them. Anyway, I have a surprise for you! Come see!"

Marlene held Lolly's hand as they skipped up the steps. I hadn't been specifically invited to join, but I hadn't been asked to leave either, so I followed them up.

We entered Marlene's room to more squealing and laughter. "Shirley!" Lolly shouted. More hugging, and jumping up and down. "When did you get back?"

"Just this morning." Shirley didn't really look like Marlene, except for a bit around the eyes and mouth. She was shorter than her sister with bobbed red hair framing her face from under a green cap.

"And look!" Shirley held out her left hand and flashed a small diamond ring.

Lolly's eyes widened, and she squealed. "Handcuffs? Theodore?"

"Yes!" Shirley said. "We're getting married!"

More jumping and exclamations. I felt like an extra thumb on a large hand. Shirley finally noticed me. "Hey," she said, "I'm Marlene's sister, Shirley."

"I'm Casey." I motioned toward her hand. "Congratulations on your engagement."

"Thanks! I'm so excited."

The three of them huddled on Marlene's bed while I sat alone on a small empty spot on Shirley's bed. Most of it was covered in clothes and boxes and accessories. Apparently, she was preparing to move out.

"When is the big day?" Lolly asked.

Shirley blushed. "Next weekend." She hurriedly added, "Theodore got a swell job on Wall Street in New York City. He even gets his very own office. He starts next week, so, that's why we have to rush. He's there now, getting us an apartment. Oh, I'm so excited to be a wife! And shopping in New York City is the cat's meow!"

I smiled and hoped I looked happy for her. She didn't know that her new husband would be losing that job within half a year, and that frivolous shopping would be a thing of the past for her and thousands of others.

Selfishly, I was glad she was getting married and moving away. It meant there was an empty bed for me once in a while, providing I could gain Marlene's friendship and come up with a good story as to why I keep disappearing.

I suddenly really, really missed Sara Watson.

Shirley hopped off the bed and started rummaging in her closet. A brown boxy suitcase with a sepia paisley interior sat open on the floor, and Shirley began filling it. I moved over to the other bed and joined Lolly and Marlene. Lolly patted my arm. "Casey here is in need of a job. Got any ideas, Marlene?"

Marlene shot me a look, and I knew I'd been right not to bring up the dancing gig. "I may know someone who could use a dishwasher."

She might have meant it as a slight, but I was happy to take a dishwashing job. Dishwashers were practically invisible, hidden from the pubic and ignored by the rest of the kitchen staff. Exactly the situation I was looking for.

"That would be great."

Marlene shrugged. "We can ankle over later."

"Hey." Lolly nuzzled close to Marlene. "Any more on your sugar daddy?"

Marlene's eyes widened in alarm. Lolly giggled. "It's okay. It's not like Casey knows him. Besides, she has a fella, right?" She turned to me. "And I can't wait to hear all about him, but first let's hear about Sheldon."

Marlene did fish motions with her lips. "I'm over Sheldon. He's too old for me anyway."

"Phonus balonus! You were goofy for him last week!"

"Well, I'm not today, Lolly. Just mind your own potatoes."

"Fine." She turned to me. "Let's hear about—what was his name? Nate?" She winked. "Does he give you good cash?"

Marlene scoffed as she eyed my chumpy dress. "I'm sure the bank's closed."

Lolly flushed. "Marlene!"

They were throwing around so much slang, I couldn't keep up. "What are you guys talking about?"

Lolly eyed me with amusement. "You really have spent too much time on the farm!"

I tried not to look offended or annoyed. I crossed my arms and pursed my lips.

Lolly wasn't good at reading body language. "C'mon. Spill."

I didn't want to talk about Nate, or anything connected

to me and my life in the future. "There's not much to tell," I said. "Pretty boring really."

Marlene laughed. "I found him interesting. And he's a regular Rudolf Valentino, Lolly. I could see that even with his beat-up face."

"Oh, Casey!" Lolly cried, obviously eager for juicy gossip. "Come on, *spill!*"

I hedged. The more lies I told, the harder it would be to keep them straight later. I really needed to downplay this. "What do you want to know?"

"How'd ya meet?"

"We met at school."

"What school do you go to?"

See! This was why I didn't want to talk about myself. I hadn't had time to research the 1920s. I was ill-equipped and unprepared!

"Johnson Lancaster?" Lolly supplied.

"Yes," I said. Why not? I had to make a note that I now attended Johnson Lancaster High School.

Lolly was like a dog with a bone. "And?"

"He plays football. I caught a wayward ball at one of his practices." Might as well stick to the real story somewhat. "That was when he'd first noticed me. I had noticed him long before that."

"Oooh. Then he asked you out?"

"Not really. We kind of hung around for a while as friends. And then eventually, we were more."

"Nice," Marlene said. "How long have you been an item?"

"A year and a half."

"That long?" Marlene said. "No wonder you act like he's old hat."

"He's not old hat. We're just...busy."

"Did he quit school too?" Lolly asked.

I tilted my head in confusion. "Quit school?"

"Ya, why you need a job?" Lolly turned to explain to Marlene. "She left the family farm to be a modern woman."

"Right. Yes. No. I mean, I quit, but Nate graduated. He goes to Boston University."

"I've heard good things about that college," Marlene said. "I've thought of going there."

Oh, man. I had to talk to her about her stocks. But it didn't look like Lolly was going to leave us alone anytime soon. She continued to pepper me with questions about Nate.

"Does he have a brother? Maybe you could introduce me?"

Nate did in fact have a brother. John was in the army in Canada, but I wasn't going to get into the complexities of that. I simply said, "No, sorry."

Lolly punched Marlene playfully in the shoulder. "I guess we gotta go find our own guys, hey?"

Marlene stood and smoothed out the wrinkles in her dress. "Let's go shopping." She walked languidly to the vanity and bent to stare at her image in the mirror. She topped off her lipstick and added another coat of mascara to her already heavily made up eyes.

"Now that you've got a fella like Nate," she said, "I suppose you don't have to worry about gettin' dolled up, huh?"

"I like to get 'dolled up'," I said, feeling defensive. "I just didn't have time to put makeup on this morning."

Marlene waved to the healthy supply of products. "Help yourself."

I thought it a good idea to try to fit in better and sat in the chair in front of the mirror to take Marlene up on her offer. Lolly jumped in to give me advice, which, I had to say, I appreciated. Girls in the twenties loved their eyeliner and wore it down past the corners of their eyes. Smokey shadows weren't reserved for the evening and Lolly coached me to put it on thick. I swiped my cheeks with a bit of blush.

"Oh, don't be shy," Lolly said, grabbing the makeup brush from me. She made two red circles on my cheeks. I almost laughed out loud at the image in the mirror. I looked like a clown.

Shirley had been busy packing this whole time. The pile of clothes in her suitcase was so high, I doubted she'd be able to close it.

"You wanna come shopping, Shirl?" Marlene asked.

"Ah, you kids go ahead. I want to finish up here."

The sidewalk outside was only wide enough for two, so I fell into third place after Marlene and Lolly. Fine by me. Kept me from having to talk about myself and spin more lies. I just had to find a way to get Marlene alone, convince her to keep her stocks and then trip back.

We visited a few small shops, which were a charming change from their modern mega mall counterparts. Marlene knew the patrons by name, and I had the feeling she gave them a lot of business. I watched as they tried dresses and hats on, and ogled over pearls and bead necklaces.

"Why don't you try something on, Casey?" Marlene

asked. She stared pointedly at my dress which I could see by now must be a few years behind in design. Fact was I didn't have any money.

"That's okay," I said. "I like watching you guys pick out things."

"She's low on scratch, remember?" Lolly said. "It's why she needs a job."

I got the feeling not many people in their circles were low on money, which made me an oddity. As if I didn't already have that going for me in spades.

"I have money on the farm," I said. "I just left so quickly, I didn't have a chance to grab it."

"I see," Marlene said. "Did you have a family quarrel?"

"You could call it that."

"Her daddy probably wants her to stay on the farm," Lolly said. She looked at me like a light bulb had just gone off. "He wants you to marry for money, don't he? Not that dapper college boy of yours, am I right? Someone old and boring, probably. "Oh, Marlene, it's so romantic. You have to help her!"

It was hard to keep up with Lolly's imagination, but I didn't see any reason to set her straight.

"Of course I'll help her," Marlene said indignantly. "We're modern women. We have the right to vote! We won't marry men we don't love to suit our fathers."

I agreed. "We sure won't!"

Marlene linked her arm with mine as we headed down the busy street. Her tone softened for the first time since I returned. "We're gonna go get you that job."

TWENTY-NINE

Despite Lolly's talk of being a modern woman, she had to head back to her farm to do afternoon chores. "I promised Pa I'd have the car back by three o'clock, but I'll come into town on the weekend," she said. "Marlene, don't forget about that party you promised to take me to."

"I haven't forgotten, darlin'."

Lolly honked and waved as she pulled away.

Lolly had been the conduit for conversation between us, and an awkward silence descended between Marlene and me. "Come on," she said, crossing the road. "If we get there early, you might be able to start tonight."

"Oh." I followed after her. Marlene wasn't as tall as me, but all that dancing had made her fit. I had to hustle to keep up.

"Hey, about the night we met," I said.

"It's fine. Your fella needed a doctor. No need to apologize again."

"Yeah, well, he said something to you I think you should ignore."

She glanced at me with curiosity. "What's that?"

"About selling your stocks. Don't listen to him. He was delirious. That knock on the head made him crazy."

"He had a point. What goes up has to come down. The bull market can't last forever. I've got a good nest egg. I'd hate to lose it."

Oh, man. This wasn't going well. "But think of how much more you could make if you left it alone. Think about your future." I hated I had to do this. If she listened to me and my loop here remained unchanged, she'd hate me forever.

Marlene changed the subject by saying, "We're here."

I looked around, confused. There wasn't a restaurant in sight. Then I saw the steps heading down to a basement-level door. I recognized it. It was the speakeasy Sheldon Vance had chased us out of.

"Are you serious?"

"Completely." She waved away my shock. "Don't worry. Sheldon never comes until after dark, and he never goes into the kitchen. Just don't take any wooden nickels and you'll be fine."

"What?"

She rolled her eyes. "Don't do anything stupid."

Good advice, but a little late in coming.

My very recent memory of dashing out of this every establishment with Sheldon Vance on my heels set my heart racing. Though it was still light outside, the basement room had no windows, and with the dim lighting and lingering smell of stale cigarette smoke, it would be easy to lose the sense of time. The only telling sign was its eerie emptiness.

Marlene strode confidently to a swinging door behind the bar and I followed her into a small dank kitchen area. A large man with a round, bald head and gray hair sprouting from a double chin glanced our way in surprise.

"Hi, Roland," Marlene said. "I brought you extra kitchen help."

Marlene spoke with an authority that surprised me. How was it that she could so confidently dictate who would work in Roland's kitchen?

"Fine," Roland said after a beat. He went back to work cleaning the fryers.

A slender boy I'd guess to be around fifteen appeared from the back. Instead of the trim barbershop cut most men and boys wore around here, he had shaggy dark hair that fell into his eyes. He stared at his shoes when Marlene introduced us. "This is Paul Junior," she said. "He's underage and comes and goes, but Roland feels sorry for him. He's an immigrant from Europe, but he won't say where. I'm not even sure if he can speak English."

"Hi, Paul Junior," I said. "Would you mind showing me what to do?"

He nodded shyly, then opened a drawer and offered me a clean apron.

"We only serve light meals," Marlene went on. "Fried kippers and clam chowder and the like, but you'll be washing a lot of glasses." She raised a knowing brow. "A lot."

"It sounds like you've done this job before."

She chortled. "I did. But only for a week. I begged Sheldon to put me on the stage. He balked at my age, but I wore him down until he let me audition. I've been on the stage ever since."

Remembering Lolly's earlier comments, I asked, "And you were never a couple?"

Marlene's red lips pulled up into smirk. "Let's just say, your instincts to run away from Sheldon are good. Now let's not talk about him anymore."

Paul Junior was a good guide. And his English was fine, though he did have a strange clip to his speech. He was shy and probably intimidated by Marlene. I wasn't surprised that he never spoke to her.

He pointed to a drawer. "The silverware is here. I polish the silver as much as I can during the slow times."

I could see the forks and knives sparkle under the kitchen lights. "Nice work."

"My father is a silversmith," he said. "I'm training as his apprentice."

"When you're not working here?" I probed.

His face flushed and he returned to staring at his shoes, which I noticed now looked oddly handmade. "True," he muttered. "When I'm not working here."

There was a back door in the kitchen that led to an alley and the garbage bins. It was also where the deliveries came, liquor in crates marked "oil" and "vinegar" or other sundry kitchen items.

Roland called for Paul Junior. "One by Land, give me a hand, will ya?"

"Why'd he call you One by Land?"

Paul Junior shrugged. "Sometimes he calls me Two by Sea. I don't know why, but he thinks it's clever."

I frowned at his comments as a strange, uncomfortable

and unwelcome awareness dawned. He returned with a heavy wooden box in his arms and grunted as he bent at the knees to lay it on the floor. "Paul Junior," I said to him, "What's your last name?"

"You mean my surname?"

"Yes, what is it?"

"Revere, miss. I'm Paul Revere Junior."

Was I staring into the eyes of another traveler? It made sense that there could be more than just Samuel, Adeline and me. If so, Paul Junior's loop ran from the 1770s to the 1920s. He came from the past, and I came from the future, but either way, neither of us belonged here.

"One if by land, two if by sea." I ducked to look the shorter boy in the eyes. "It's a quote made famous by your father."

His eyes flickered. "You mean my great-great-great grandfather."

I didn't want to freak him out, and I didn't have time to get into what we may have in common. I didn't blame him for not wanting to tell the truth. And maybe he was telling the truth. Maybe he was the great-great-great grandson of Paul Revere.

But...wouldn't he be aware of that famous quote, then? The only way a Bostonian could get through his first fifteen years of life and not hear that story a billion times is if it hadn't happened yet for him.

I eyed him suspiciously, but turned to Roland's gruff voice when he called. "Casey, you'll be working between the kitchen and the bar. Ask Vivian what to do."

I reluctantly left Paul Junior and went to the blond woman leaning against the service side of the bar. "Are you

Vivian?" I asked. She looked at me as she butted out a cigarette and blew smoke from the side of her mouth. I noticed the room was starting to fill up. A brass band rehearsed on the stage.

"Are ya new kitchen crew?" she asked with a husky voice. I nodded.

"Good. The girls will be here shortly. Make sure the bar is stocked with clean glasses, and pick up dirty ones off the tables. Try to stay out of the customers' way."

I assumed "the girls" were the scantily clad waitresses who walked the room with trays of drinks. "I'm here to help," I said.

Vivian cast me a bored glance then waved to someone across the room. "Darling!" she cried. "You came! So good to see you!"

THIRTY

THE LATER IT GOT, the busier it got. I worked up a sweat running between the kitchen and the bar. Paul Junior reminded me to take off my apron before doing the rounds to clear the tables. I didn't know exactly how classy I looked in my costume, a 1920s look-alike, and a shiny, red face.

The jazz band was top-notch and when I had a spare moment to enjoy them, I nodded my head and tapped a foot in time. All the musicians were black, I noticed, even though none of the patrons were.

The place was packed shoulder-to-shoulder, well-dressed couples laughing and drinking, blowing smoke into the air. I couldn't believe the Boston Police Department didn't know about this place. How could they not see the stream of bodies making their way here after dusk?

Marlene stopped at the bar and lifted a finger to Vivian. Vivian's eyes twitched at the corners as she poured a drink into a glass and pushed it to Marlene.

"Thanks Vivian," Marlene said dryly. Vivian turned her back to Marlene before making a dirty face.

Marlene didn't seem to notice Vivian's attitude, and if she did, she didn't seem to care. She took a large swallow of whatever liquor was in her glass and let out a throaty sigh.

Then she asked, "How's it going back there?"

I glanced back at Paul Junior who stood at the door to the kitchen. "Good."

Marlene walked to the back of the room behind the stage and disappeared. I returned to the kitchen, tied my apron back on, and helped Paul Junior wash up more glasses. He was careful not to catch my eye longer than necessary, and it was too noisy to talk about anything serious anyway. Besides, I never knew when Roland would suddenly appear. He took a lot of smoke breaks in the back alley, watching out for new deliveries.

I ventured back to the main room, just as the dancers lined up on stage, all Caucasian, and I spotted Marlene in the center with the largest feathers sprouting from her headband. I was starting to see how a rich Marlene would be very influential. Only a few years older than me, she was rapidly working her way up the social ladder of this underground society.

When the dancers left the stage, the band returned, and the floor filled with couples doing the Charleston and other types of swing dances. It made me think of Nate and our time together here just a couple days ago.

My heart squeezed tightly with remorse. If only I hadn't gone to Hollywood and kissed the nearest boy in a fit of childish anger. If I'd only stayed calm and trusted Nate, none of this would've happened. I had to fix things. Fix the time-line. Fix what was broken between Nate and me.

The dancers ended their set to loud hooting and applause. Marlene soaked up the attention with her arms stretched out into the air, a bare knee bent in and lips coated in dark red spread into a bright smile. A short while later, she approached the bar, changed from her dance suit and dressed in a fabulous, sparkly and expensive flapper dress.

"Hey, Casey," she said loudly through the noise.

"Great routine," I shouted back.

"Thanks. It was fun."

"Looked it. By the way, thanks again for the job."

"It's nifty. My sister left for New York, so you can have her bed if you want for tonight."

I smiled with relief. "That would be great."

Vivian pushed another glass to Marlene, and Marlene sauntered over to a table in the far back corner. I shivered when I saw who was sitting there, and impulsively ducked low behind the bar. Sheldon Vance. I should've known he'd show up eventually. He must've arrived just before the danc-ing. I would've spotted him sooner otherwise.

I couldn't keep from watching him and Marlene. Marlene said they weren't a couple, but they were sitting pretty close together and leaning toward each other as they talked. They were laughing and smiling. Maybe he *was* her sugar daddy and she was ashamed to admit it? Had he bought her that beautiful dress?

I had to know what they were talking about. I picked up a tray and started collecting dirty glasses, working my way toward their table, but careful to keep my back to them. I hovered around a table close by and caught snippets of their conversation.

"Sheldon darling, I think I'm going to sell my stocks..."

"Don't be crazy. Now's the time to buy more, not sell. It's a bull market. Don't you wanna be stinking rich?"

Awesome. Sheldon Vance was doing my job for me.

"You know I do," Marlene returned, "but some are saying it's going to crash."

"What? Where'd you hear that? It's just fearmongering, doll. The economy couldn't be better. Don't you worry your pretty little head."

I couldn't help but sneak a peek. I held my breath. Marlene and Sheldon were locking lips! He had to be at least ten years older than her.

Just then Sheldon's eyes opened and his dark gaze pierced mine. He pulled sharply away from Marlene.

"Hey!" he exclaimed loudly over the noise in the room.

I tried to get out of his sight, but the clientele who filled the crowded space slowed my progress.

"Excuse me, pardon me, I need to get through..." I pushed my way past several annoyed guests. A girl spilled her drink on her dress and shouted, "Bushwa!"

A strong hand gripped my arm and I knew I'd been caught. I turned toward Sheldon Vance and swallowed.

"What are you doing here?" he growled.

"Cleaning tables?"

Smirking, he said, "You came a long way just to serve tables."

"Well, I've always been an East Coast girl."

"Why are you working *here*? Are you spying on me?"

He leaned closer, and I felt his hot breath against my neck. "You plan on turnin' me or my establishment in?"

"No!" I didn't know if it was a good idea to point out that Marlene got me the job. I didn't want to get her into trouble with Sheldon. "I'm just here to make money."

He narrowed his eyes into nasty dark slits. "How'd you get outta jail?"

I was getting tired of being bullied by him and snapped back, "How'd *you* get out of jail?"

His jaw tightened, along with his hold on my arm. "You just keep your pretty mouth shut. I'm not going back to the slammer because of a dumb dame like you." He leaned in to whisper loudly in my ear. I cringed as his hot breath blasted against my cheek. "I'm watching you. You cause me any trouble, say anything about my 'movie,' and you'll be sorry you were ever born."

I tugged my arm free from his grip. His coal-dark eyes flashed with evil, and I didn't waste any time getting away from him. I ran toward the kitchen, dodging couples dancing, and barmaids balancing trays full of drinks held high above their heads. I felt dizzy and hurried to the kitchen, away from the crowd of partiers and out of Sheldon's field of vision. I didn't want him to see me disappear into thin air.

I escaped Sheldon but forgot about Paul Junior. His startled, wide-eyed stare was the last thing I saw before hitting the tunnel of light.

THIRTY-ONE

IT WAS dark outside and cold. I stood, panting, across the street from the apartment building where I lived with my mom. There was no fire, no policemen or firemen. The streets were quiet and isolated. I shivered, alone on the sidewalk, dismayed by the fact that I once again wore only a tank top and PJ shorts under a light jacket.

I could sense that things were different. I just couldn't tell how. Had the timeline been correct or, heaven forbid, was I on a completely new timeline? I raced across the street and pulled on the door. It didn't budge, and I'd left the burning building without a key. I hated the thought of waking my mom up in the middle of the night to let me in. I couldn't think of an excuse as to why I was out and undressed that would be believable.

I searched for the button that had our last name—Donovan—but couldn't find it. It used to be the fourth one from the top in the column on the right. I squinted. Not there. Had our name shifted? A thorough check confirmed what I already had guessed. I didn't live here anymore.

This was good! Hopefully it meant I lived in my house with my whole family again. Unfortunately, it meant I'd have to traipse all the way across town.

Walking alone half-dressed after dark wasn't a smart thing to do. I dug through my backpack, relieved to find my cell phone there. I almost called Nate, but I remembered how he looked at me when he said we had to go back and fix things together. I didn't feel like explaining everything that had happened. I brought up Lucinda's name and pressed call.

Three rings then she answered with a sleepy hello.

"Lucinda? It's Casey." I held my breath. Did she know me? Were we friends?"

"Hey, Casey. What's up? Why are you calling so late?"

I almost burst into tears. "We're still best friends?"

"Of course we are. Hey, I overreacted about your California tripper friend. Sorry. You're allowed to have new friends. I have them, too. I was being stupid."

"You don't know how happy I am right now!"

She paused before asking, "Casey? Is something wrong?"

"Something *was* wrong, but I think it might be right now. But I need a favor. I need you to come pick me up."

"Where are you?"

I gave her the address.

"What on earth are you doing there?"

"It's a long story. I'll tell you all about it on the drive home."

"I'm getting dressed as we speak."

I rubbed my forehead, trying to work out the headache

that had developed over the course of the evening. "This is going to sound like a strange question, Luce, but can you tell me where I live?"

"Oh, God, Casey. You have amnesia? And I'm the only one you remember? BFF for the win! Don't worry, I'm leaving right now. See you in fifteen."

Okay. I guess I'd find out where I live soon enough. I huddled in the alcove of the apartment entrance and hummed a tune to pass the time. I got a little too animated with a Taylor Swift impression and swiped a hand through sticky silk.

"*Ew!*" I jumped back, wildly brushing the web and any spiders from my hands.

A car pulled up, blinding me with its headlights.

Lucinda rolled down her window and called out. "Nice dance!"

"Ha ha," I said, racing for the warmth of her car. I squeezed in and rubbed my legs. "Turn the heat up."

Lucinda pushed the lever to red. Her gaze took in my lack of clothing. "So... pajama party gone wrong?"

I ignored the taunt. "Something happened when I was in Hollywood."

"I know. You kissed Austin King." Lucinda pulled out into the street. I had about twenty minutes to tell her everything.

"That's not all that happened. I was so upset about cheating on Nate like that, I triggered a trip. At the same time, Adeline had been fighting with her boyfriend, and she triggered a trip. When I ran away from Austin, I ran into Adeline."

"Oh my God," Lucinda said, anticipating what I was about to say. "You didn't..."

"We did. We went back in time together. Only my loop was to 1863 and hers was to 1956."

"Which one did you go to?"

"Neither." I paused for effect. "We went somewhere new for both of us. 1929."

Lucinda gasped. "1929? Seriously?"

"Super seriously."

"What happened?" She stared at me wide-eyed for so long, I had to motion to her to keep her eyes on the road. Then I told her about getting conned into helping the Vance brothers rob a bank. "It's so stupid."

"And they arrested you?"

"Handcuffs and everything."

Lucinda shook her head with disbelief. "Casey, you live the wildest life."

"I haven't even gotten to the good part yet."

She exhaled. "Okay, lay it on me. What's the good part?"

"We tripped back to our present, to the party at Bluebell's and no one knew we'd left. Except someone had been taking pictures of me and Austin, beyond the kissing one, making it look like we'd been flirting and hanging out a lot, when mostly I was glaring at Austin and trying to get away from him."

"Who'd do that? And why?"

"My gut says Fiona's behind it somehow."

"But," Lucinda squinted in thought. "She was in Spain. That's a pretty long reach."

"She hired someone. I wouldn't put it past her. Desperate people do desperate things."

"Hired who?"

"Spike, maybe. He never spoke two words to me the whole trip."

"That just proves he's shy."

I shrugged. "Or devious. Anyway, I tripped back in time again, this time with Nate."

"Here in Cambridge."

"Yeah. He was so mad my loop had rerouted to 1929."

"Yeah, I'm kind of mad, too. The Watson family watched out for you. It was comforting for me to know. Now who's going to take care of you?"

"I take care of myself, Luce."

"I know that. I just meant..."

"I know what you meant. Sorry, I just feel so guilty that this situation happened in the first place. Anyway, this is the part you're not going to believe. When Nate and I returned from 1929 to the present, our timeline had *changed*."

"*Changed?* What do you mean?"

"I mean, my parents were separated. I lived in that apartment building with my mom, and you and I weren't friends."

Her mouth dropped open. "What? Is that why you were stuck on the other side of town?"

"Yes."

"So, how...?"

"I tripped back to 1929 again, without Nate this time, and tried to fix things."

Lucinda pulled into the drive of my house, the same one from before. Tim's car sat in the driveway. I let out a long breath. "It looks like it worked."

Lucinda cut the engine and stared at me. "You've been busy."

"And I'm exhausted."

"Well, go get some sleep and promise me you'll try to stay put for a while. I, for one, am happy with things the way they are now. I don't want you to go changing things."

"Believe me, I don't want to change things either."

Except for the distance that had grown between Nate and me. *That* I wanted changed.

"Thanks for coming for me, Luce. I owe you one."

"I think you owe me more than one by now."

I chuckled. "I suppose you're right."

"Thanks for the Sparks Notes version of events," Lucinda said. "I'll call you tomorrow and you can fill me in on all the details."

I tiptoed through my house, pausing to do a little happy dance when I confirmed that everything looked just the way I'd left it—lived-in messiness, but not too messy, all the same furniture and pictures on the wall, Dad's coats in the closet, Tim's backpack by the door. I eased up the steps, avoiding the creaky spots, and slipped into my bedroom. Sleep claimed me hard and fast, and I even dreamed I was snoring.

My alarm startled me awake. I hadn't set it, but a version of me must have. I wouldn't have minded a few more hours, but it was a school day, and I couldn't afford to get behind if I wanted to graduate with honors.

I lumbered dutifully to the shower and enjoyed the hot water and the modern plumbing. We had so much simple luxury in this century I never wanted to take it for granted.

I found Tim in the kitchen when I went looking for breakfast. I squeezed him from behind. "It's so good to see you!"

"Hey," he said. "I'm trying to butter my toast here." He

watched me as I moved to our massive fridge and pulled out the giant jug of milk. I poured it into my cereal and took a bite.

Tim grinned. "Okay, spit it out."

"The milk?" I said coyly. "I don't think Mom would appreciate that."

"You're a comedian. Did you and Nate have *fun* last night?" He winked. "That would explain your good mood."

I scowled at him and felt my joy at returning home ebb. Nate and I did not have *fun* last night. We hadn't had *fun* in a long time, but I wasn't going to tell my brother that. I picked up my cereal bowl and took it upstairs. I passed Mom in the hall.

"Good morning," she said before disappearing into her office. I grinned. Take that, Bretton Wiles Interiors.

I closed the door to my room and situated myself on my bed, careful not to spill any milk. I thought about Nate as I finished my breakfast. I had to do something for him. To show him how sorry I was and how much I cared about him and that I wanted to make things right between us.

The question was what?

THIRTY-TWO

I BARELY HAD my teeth brushed when I heard Lucinda honking her horn. I sneaked a quick look in the mirror. I wore jeans with sneakers and a plaid button-down shirt. I suddenly was unsure about my choice, but I didn't have time to change my mind. I snatched my jacket and purse off my desk chair and hurried down the stairs.

"I'm going, Mom!" I shouted. Her voice filtered after me, "Have a good day!"

I hopped into Lucinda's idling car. She glared at me and pointed to her face, "If these bags don't go away by the time I meet up with Sam, you are in big trouble."

I laughed. "Hey, my bags are no better."

Lucinda examined her eyes in her rearview mirror before checking over her shoulder and backing out of my driveway. "Have you talked to him yet?" Lucinda asked.

I knew she meant Nate, and my pulse quickened. "No, not yet. I'm afraid, Luce."

Her jaw dropped. "Of what? Nate loves you." She

reached over and patted my arm. "One stupid little mistake can't change that."

I hoped she was right. I smiled to reassure her that I was okay. "Eyes on the road, Luce."

Sam was already waiting for Lucinda at the school parking lot. I waved her off, remembering all the times she had done the same for me when Nate was a student here. I maneuvered down the busy hallways to my locker and searched for the books I needed. Nate used to always lean against the neighboring locker, taking me in with interest when I dug through my things. He didn't think I noticed him watching me, but I had, and I loved it. I stared at the locker door, imaging him there.

It was my turn to make the big gesture, but what? Guys have lots of choices when shopping for girls: flowers, chocolates, jewelry, but what does a girl get for a guy? Beef jerky?

The first bell brought me to my senses, and I hurried to my next class. I hadn't even had a chance to check in with Adeline. I wanted to make sure there were no shifts of change for her. I texted as I walked.

Casey: I'm back and timeline seems restored on my end. How's it with you?

She didn't respond right away, and then I remembered she was three hours behind and probably still sleeping.

I plowed into a body, and my books tumbled to the floor.

"I'm so sorry..." I began, then I saw who it was. "Oh, it's you."

Austin King crouched beside me, picking up one of my stray textbooks. "Hey, you ran into me."

We stood at the same time, and Austin placed the book

on my pile. He grinned crookedly and saluted as he walked backward, away from me. "See you around, Donovan."

I couldn't wait for the school day to end. I was both eager and nervous to see Nate, and that was the only after-school activity I had planned. I drank extra coffee at lunch to ward off the yawning fits my traveling jaunt had caused. Sam joined Lucinda and me at our table at lunchtime and despite the way he sprawled out in his chair like a drowsy dog, and the way he kept his hand possessively on Lucinda's leg, I decided to give him the benefit of the doubt. Innocent until proven guilty and all that.

Austin sat with his buddies at a table by the window. A new girl with wavy auburn hair sat to his right. She gazed up at him through fluttering eyelashes, and I worried she might drop to her knees in worship. He caught me looking and cocked a brow. I rolled my eyes.

Misha sat alone with a textbook opened in front of her, but her interest didn't lie in whatever was written there. Her eyes were locked in on someone across the room from her. I followed the path of her gaze. Of course.

I excused myself to Lucinda, went to Misha and pulled out a chair. She startled when she saw me and nervously pushed up on her glasses.

"Oh, hi, Casey," she said. "How are things?"

"I expect you know," I said. Even though I'd been extremely busy with other more pressing things, the whole photo mystery had worked itself out in the background. It wasn't too hard, really, to figure out who was present when all those compromising photos had been taken. I just didn't understand why until now.

"Is it because of Austin? You like him, but he liked me?"

Misha blanched. "I don't know what you're talking about."

"The photos, Misha. You took the pictures of me and Austin together on the Hollywood trip and posted them online."

Misha's expression hardened. "So what if I did? You had Nate Mackenzie and that wasn't enough. No, you had to have Austin, too! At first I thought, since we shared a room and were sort of friends, that maybe he'd notice me. That his interest would shift from you—not available—to me, available. But no matter what I did, I stayed invisible like always."

"If you were trying to hurt Austin," I said. "I don't think it worked."

"I wasn't trying to hurt Austin," she hissed. "I was trying to hurt *you*. You're beautiful and smart, with not one but *two* hot guys crazy about you. It's not fair."

Her venom shocked me. "I'm sorry you feel this way."

She squinted at me. "Did it work?"

"Did what work?"

"Did I hurt you?"

I blinked. "Yes."

Misha shifted her chair back, grabbed her books and her tray of lunch trash. She smirked back at me. "Good."

I watched her storm away, and instead of feeling angry, I felt pity.

Once she disappeared, my eye was drawn to the window where a lunchtime ball game was going on outside. A tall, dark-haired guy was up to bat. I squinted against the light. Tim?

I was perplexed and a little worried. There was no way Tim could run with his bad leg. What did he think he was doing? The pitcher let the ball go, and I heard the faint "thwack" through the open window. The ball went high and long. Someone else ran the bases. I found myself cheering along with Tim as the runner, hit first, second, third, and then slid into home seconds before the ball slapped into the catcher's mitt.

I felt a smile stretch across my face. Way to go, Tim! I loved how he was making the most out of life, not letting his disability get in his way. His can-do attitude pushed the foggy effect of Misha's vindictiveness out of my mind. Suddenly, I knew exactly what I wanted to do for Nate. I was going to make things between us right again.

THIRTY-THREE

LUCINDA and I were mall junkies. There wasn't a shop in the massive two-story complex that I didn't know about. I rode the escalator to the top floor, getting off by the food court. The corner of my mouth lifted up as I remembered meeting Nate there, tripping back to the nineteenth century together and then watching his public breakup with his evil girlfriend, Jessica Fuller. She'd verbally attacked me, and he came to my defense. It marked a major turning point for us.

There was a little clock shop that also did a bit of shoe repair. It was tucked incongruously down a narrow hall behind Build-a-Bear.

An elderly gentleman worked quietly behind a wooden counter. He wore loose trousers held up with suspenders. His white hair was slicked back, and he watched me over the top of narrow spectacles perched on a long nose.

"Can I help you?"

"I'm looking for a pocket watch."

He shuffled to one of the glass cases in the shop and pointed to a selection under the glass.

There were several in varying degrees of condition. I pointed to a brass one in the center. "How old is it?"

The man opened the case and removed the watch popping the ornate cover open. A long chain hung from the hinge and he wrapped his fingers through it while laying the piece on his hand. "This one originates from the mid 1800s."

Perfect. A reminder to us both where our love story began. "Does it work?"

He wound the pin and handed the watch to me. It felt cool, and heavier than it looked. I held it to my ear and grinned at the ticking sound.

"Can you engrave it for me?"

The old man shrugged. Sure.

The cost of the watch wiped out my savings account, but I knew I'd done the right thing. Nate would love this.

The man wrapped the watch in thick white tissue. I pushed it into my pocket before reaching into my purse for my phone. I took a deep breath and sent Nate a text.

Casey: Hi! It's me. Missing you. XXXOO :)

I didn't have to wait long for Nate's response. I was hoping for a "Miss you too," or "Can't wait to see you," or even "Let's talk soon." My heart sunk when I read his cold reply.

Nate: You went back without me.

Casey: I can't control these things. Please can we talk?

Nate: I'm home now.

Casey: I'm on my way.

My heart knocked around in my chest as the bus drew to a stop down the street from Nate's house. I took a long breath, smoothed my shirt and ran MY fingers through my curls. I removed the watch from my pocket, opened the tissue and took another look at the engraving.

Nate & Casey
Love that transcends Time

I WRAPPED the watch back up, holding it in one hand as I prepared to knock. My knuckles never reached the door. It suddenly opened, and Nate filled the frame. He was freshly showered and clean-shaven. The sporty scent of his after-shave wafted to me and made my heart sputter.

"Hi," I said.

"Hi." Nate closed the door behind him and joined me outside. "My mom's home," he said, as an explanation as to why he hadn't invited me in.

"How is she?"

"She's good. Trim figure. Hair clean and salon-styled. That was how I knew you'd gone back. One moment she was frumpy house wife, and the next, top-selling realtor."

"I didn't mean to go back without you," I said.

"I know, Casey. I know there are things you can't control."

"The main thing is the timeline is fixed," I said quickly.

"Marlene didn't sell her stocks before the crash. You're here, and I'm here, and we're here together."

I reached for his hand and held it tight. "I love you, Nate. I'm so sorry for what happened in Hollywood, and I promise you, nothing like that will ever, ever happen again." I leaned in close and stared up into his pale green eyes. "Please, will you forgive me?"

Nate's chin dropped, and his gaze broke from mine. My nerves shot off like party sparklers, waiting for him to speak. I gripped the pocket watch tightly.

Nate lifted his head and met my gaze. "I forgive you, Casey, but I can't go on with you."

What? WHAT? My eyes fluttered like a butterfly with a damaged wing. My mouth grew dry. "Wh-what do you mean?"

"I mean, I think it's time we moved on from each other."

No. This wasn't how it was supposed to go. We were supposed to kiss and make up!

I shook my head sharply. "I don't want to move on. Nate, please, it was just one stupid kiss."

"I've done stupid things, too, Casey, but I've always been loyal to you." He sighed. "You're young. You need to experience things. You should know what it's like to kiss guys other than me. You should know what it's like to play the field. Be single and carefree. Somewhere along the line, we turned into an old married couple. We moved too fast."

The earth beneath me shifted. I couldn't breathe. I was feeling full-blown panic. "No! I don't agree. I don't want to kiss any other guys. I don't want to play the field. I need you."

"But that's the thing," he said softly. "You don't need me. You're strong, resilient and resourceful. You've proven that time and time again."

A whimper escaped my lips. "Nate?" I held out his gift, but my sweaty palms had soaked the tissue, and it just looked like a big wad of used Kleenex.

"Our time is up, Casey." He brushed his lips against my cheek and whispered, "Good-bye."

As he disappeared into his house, I was slammed with a bolt of dizziness and swallowed by a tunnel of bright light.

TO BE CONTINUED....

I HOPE you enjoyed reading COUNTER CLOCKWISE. If you'd like to on leestraussbooks.com, I'd love to hear what you thought! Reviews are really helpful to authors and help readers find the books they love.

Don't miss the Final Clockwise Collection book!
CLOCKWORK CRAZY

THE CLOCKWISE COLLECTION FINALE!

The stress created by Casey's recent split from Nate causes her to trip back in time in a haphazard manner, and not always to the same time! Sometimes she's in 1929 Boston getting more entangled than ever with the mishaps of her new and not-so-helpful friends, and at other times she's back in 1775 trying to make sure the colonists still win the war of Independence!

Will the craziness ever stop? And will she and Nate work out things in time for graduation?

From USA Today bestselling author Lee Strauss.

What readers are saying: " Didn't want it to end!" "Great Final Book to the Clockwork Series" " A wonderful conclusion"

. . .

Shop at leestraussbooks.com

Read on for an excerpt!

CLOCKWORK CRAZY
(The Clockwise Collection #6)
By Lee Strauss

CHAPTER ONE

It's better to have love and lost then to never have loved at all.

What a bunch of crock!

And the old adage was certainly no comfort to me as I
curled up in the middle of some random farmers' field,
bawling my eyes out. I snotted up my sleeve as groans
sounding eerily similar to that of an injured beast erupted
from my esophagus.

I wanted to curse every silly love song and romantic solil-
oquy I'd ever heard. The people who penned those words
were *liars*. Heart break was explosive, wrenching, and anni-

hilating. It battered, and whipped and taunted the one afflicted by it. It crushed me like an avalanche of ragged stones without the decency to actually kill me. The pain was so deep and thorough I felt like someone was peeling off my skin.

I hated, hated, *hated* that I had known love. It was so much better for me when love was an unattainable dream, a fairytale, a pleasant stroking of my imagination. I wished with all my bruised and bleeding heart that I'd never stopped *hating* Nate.

This present agony was all his fault! If he hadn't accepted a dare to dance with me at that stupid Fall Dance (I take back the forgiveness I'd extended to Lucinda for tricking me into going), and hadn't tripped with me back to the 19th Century, and hadn't let my infatuation turn into love and worse, if he hadn't loved me back—I'd be happily unaware of this torment and probably half-heartedly dating Austin King. I'd be graduating in a few weeks with my body, soul and spirit in one piece and in wonderful ignorance.

Ignorance was *totally* underrated.

What you don't know won't hurt you—how true! I wanted to start a campaign to warn other high school girls: study, get good grades and for God's sake, leave the boys alone!

"Casey?"

I'd been so tangled up in my ball of woe, I hadn't heard anyone approach. I quickly wiped my face with the bottom of my shirt, dabbed at my eyes and drew my fingers through my ran-away curls. I turned to the female voice and gawked at Marlene Charter's friend Lolly.

"Casey, is that you? Are you all right?"

I jumped to my feet and brushed the dirt off my jeans. I kept my eyes averted. "Yeah. I'm okay." A hiccup betrayed me.

She shook her messy brunette bob. "Those are the strangest work clothes I've ever seen."

I could barely think in my emotional state. Right, I was in 1929 wearing a striped red and navy blue T-shirt, skinny jeans, and canvas running shoes. My school pack lay at my feet. Unfortunately, it only contained my homework and not any costumes for this period.

Lolly wore oversized field trousers held up with suspenders and a blue button-down blouse. Two furry mid-sized mutts sniffed the ground around us. A tractor was parked in the distance.

My hands were empty and I inhaled sharply. Nate's pocket watch was missing. I must've dropped it. I fell back to my knees and examine the ground around me, turning over stones and pushing aside some variety of plantation.

"Are you looking for something?" Lolly asked.

A thorough search of my immediate surroundings proved that it hadn't traveled with me. I must've dropped it on Nate's front step.

"I thought I'd dropped something, but..." I brushed soil off my knees as I stood up. "Is this your farm?" I asked. I was used to serendipity and chance in my way of life, so the fact that Lolly stood in front of me just now almost didn't surprise me.

"Yeah. How'd you find it? Were you looking for me?"

I sniffed and turned away to take in the open pastures and farmland that would one day be the neighborhood Nate Mackenzie moved in to.

"I'm kind of lost."

"Forgive me, but you do look it. Why don't you come back to the house with me and you can tell me what's wrong. And please don't insult my intelligence by saying that there's nothing wrong. You look a mess, darlin'."

She whistled for the dogs and started toward the tractor. I picked up my modern backpack and followed.

"It's a one seater," she said, hoping on to the wide seat, "but it's big enough for you to slip in behind me."

I placed my foot on a runner and heaved myself up behind Lolly. The tractor stuttered and popped as Lolly turned the engine over, stepped on the clutch and put it into gear. We puttered toward a farmhouse in the distance and I was glad the motor was too loud to talk over. I had approximately five minutes to get my story straight before Lolly began her interrogation. Though I've only known her for a short time, I knew her well enough to know she would be relentless in her quest for answers.

We approached a small farmhouse painted canary yellow. Large trees in a sea of leafy green, surrounded it like a big protective hug. Several out-buildings—sheds, barn, outhouse, sat just beyond. Lolly pulled the tractor into a shady spot behind one of them and killed the engine.

"We'll have to sneak you upstairs and get you out of those rags," she said. "Ma's very conservative and won't appreciate that you're wearing dungarees that are much, much too small for you. Though," she added with a sympathetic glance at my clothing choice, "you can't be to blame if you've outgrown your work clothes and your family can't afford to buy you new ones that fit properly. Did you say you were the eldest?"

I didn't remember what I'd told her and Marlene about my family. I'd learn it was best to stick with the truth whenever possible.

"Yes."

"I know you've been crying and once we're ready, you're going to tell me all about it."

I didn't have a chance to ask her, "Ready for what?"

A line of laundry hung in the back yard with large white sheets floating in the breeze like sails. Lolly ducked low as we followed along and motioned for me to do the same. "In case Ma's looking out the window," Lolly explained.

Lolly carefully opened a screen door, nodded with her head that I should enter first, and then she slowly let the door close without a sound. I had the feeling Lolly was skilled and experienced at sneaking in and out of her house.

We paused at the base of a narrow flight of stairs.

"Follow my steps exactly," Lolly whispered. She strategically placed her foot one side of a step and then the other—sometimes in the middle, a pattern that got us to the second floor without a squeak.

We stepped inside a small bedroom with ceilings that sloped sharply to the windows. There was only a short strip where I could stand up straight and not bump my head. Lolly chuckled. "It's helps that I'm short. At least when it comes to getting dressed in this room."

Despite its diminutive size, the room was cozy, with floral wallpaper that ran from the wood floor to the cream-colored ceiling. White sheers floated lazily around the opened windows. Lolly opened a dark wardrobe that rested against the longest portion of an interior wall and removed a couple dresses. She held a flowing, tangerine and peach one out to me.

"I hope it fits," she said. "It drops to my ankles on me, so it should easily fall to your shins."

She unabashedly stripped out of her farm trousers revealing a conservative set of undergarments that would blush at the sight of my comparatively skimpy under things. There wasn't much I could do about that and Lolly was already busy in font of her vanity mirror, fixing her hair, that I didn't think she'd notice. I slipped out of my jeans and t-shirt, pushed them under Lolly's bed with my toe and wiggled into Lolly's dress. We were both of slender build and the loose style made way for any differences in body shape, and as Lolly predicted the dress landed at my shins.

"Can I borrow brush and a few pins?" I asked. I ducked to get a glimpse of myself in the mirror and stared at my blotchy face and bloodshot eyes. No matter how badly I felt right now, I had to stop crying, at least until I was home again and in the privacy of my own room.

Lolly pointed to all her hair accessories, "Sure thing."

I remembered how Adeline had made a faux bob out of my long hair, the first time we'd tripped back to 1929 in Hollywood. My version wasn't nearly as neat, but it would do. My real problem wasn't my hair, but my feet. There was no way my clodhoppers would fit into any of Lolly's petite shoes.

I pointed a toe. "I'm going to have to go barefoot." Unless I wore my sneakers.

Lolly's eyes widened in shock at my pronouncement. I gathered a lady without stockings or footwear was even a little too much for this "modern" girl.

"My mother has large feet too—I take after my father's side of the family," she added quickly. Before saying more she disappeared out of the room. I took the opportunity to dig into her cosmetics, knowing from my previous encounter that Lolly wouldn't mind. In fact, I knew she'd insist, and for the first time I wondered where were getting ready to go out to. I packed it on to even out my skin tone and hoped that plenty of eye makeup would detract from the puffiness.

Lolly returned with a really unattractive pair of brown tie up shoes—very sensible. She smiled apologetically. "Sorry, this is the best she has."

"It's fine," I said. It wasn't like I was trying to impress anyone, anyway. "I assume we're going somewhere?"

"Marlene's throwing a party. I promised her I'd come. Won't she be surprised to see you again!"

"Won't she!" I said it with a touch of sarcasm. Marlene was probably less than impressed that I "took off" before finishing my shift at the speak easy. Not only was poor Paul Junior left alone to do all the clean up, he was probably freaked out at seeing me disappear into thin air like that.

Lolly handed me a strand of long beads, and I slipped them over my head. She looked at me like I was a project she wasn't quite finished with but didn't know what else to do. "Let's go."

I followed her exact pattern down the steps to the back door. She opened it and motioned me to go outside. "I'll be right there," she whispered. "Stay out of sight."

"Ma!" she called. "I'm going into town."

"Lolita! You hold on now!" A moment later her mother's voice filtered outside again. "You're not going into town dressed like that!"

"Ma, we've been through this a hundred times. This is how young adults dress nowadays."

"It just makes you look so... cheap. Did you forget that Thomas Burgess is coming for dinner tonight? I need your help to prepare things."

"Thomas? Again? Ma...."

"Lolita, don't you lip me!"

"But, Pa promised I could have the car to go into town today."

"Fine, go if you must, but be home by five o'clock, do you hear? I mean it young lady."

The door slammed and Lolly scurried past me in a huff. I hurried after her. "Is everything all right?"

"No! We're not going to be able to stay for Marlene's party. She's going be so angry!"

We came to a narrow garage and I recognized the jalopy inside. I climbed into the passenger seat. Once Lolly had backed us out safely, I asked "Who's Thomas?"

"He's the farmer's son next door. Our parents want to join our farms because they think it's the only way to make the most of the booming economy. The truth is, we bought too many new tractors and machinery with easy money from the bank. They're more expensive to run and alone we can't produce fast enough to make the loan payments."

"What do you mean by join the farms? They want you to marry him?"

"Yes. I'm an only child and a girl. My parents wanted a lot of kids, but...well, they only got me, unfortunately. We have to hire out help, but cash flow isn't there for that. Thomas is one of ten kids, and the next up eligible to marry." She let out a long, sad sigh. "He's a nice enough fellow, but I don't love him." She pressed her shoulders back. "I'm not going to marry him. I'm a modern girl!"

Lolly geared down as she came to the intersection at the main road into Boston. "Now, enough about me," she said with an arched brow. "Why were you crying your eyes out in the middle of my field?"

End Sample

Shop at leestraussbooks.com

ABOUT THE AUTHOR

Lee Strauss is a USA TODAY bestselling author of The Ginger Gold Mysteries series, The Higgins & Hawke Mystery series, The Rosa Reed Mystery series (cozy historical mysteries), A Nursery Rhyme Mystery series (mystery suspense), The Light & Love series (sweet romance), The Clockwise Collection (YA time travel romance), and young adult historical fiction with over a million books read. She has titles published in German and French, and a growing audio library.

When Lee's not writing or reading she likes to cycle, hike, and stare at the ocean. She loves to drink caffè lattes and red wines in exotic places, and eat dark chocolate anywhere.

For more info on books by Lee Strauss and her social media links, visit leestraussbooks.com. To make sure you don't miss the next new release, be sure to sign up for her readers' list!

Discuss the books, ask questions, share your opinions. Fun giveaways! Join the Lee Strauss Readers' Group on Facebook for more info.

Did you know you can follow your favourite authors on Bookbub? If you subscribe to Bookbub — (and if you don't, why don't you? - They'll send you daily emails alerting you to sales and new releases on just the kind of books you like to read!) — follow me to make sure you don't miss the next Ginger Gold Mystery!

www.leestraussbooks.com
leestraussbooks@gmail.com

MORE FROM LEE STRAUSS

Shop at leestraussbooks.com

GINGER GOLD MYSTERY SERIES (cozy 1920s historical)

Cozy. Charming. Filled with Bright Young Things. This Jazz Age murder mystery will entertain and delight you with its 1920s flair and pizzazz!

Murder on the SS Rosa

Murder at Hartigan House

Murder at Bray Manor

Murder at Feathers & Flair

Murder at the Mortuary

Murder at Kensington Gardens

Murder at St. George's Church

The Wedding of Ginger & Basil

Murder Aboard the Flying Scotsman

Murder at the Boat Club

Murder on Eaton Square

Murder by Plum Pudding

Murder on Fleet Street

Murder at Brighton Beach

Murder in Hyde Park

Murder at the Royal Albert Hall

Murder in Belgravia

Murder on Mallowan Court

Murder at the Savoy

Murder at the Circus

Murder in France

Murder at Yuletide

Murder at Madame Tussauds

LADY GOLD INVESTIGATES (Ginger Gold companion short stories)

Volume 1

Volume 2

Volume 3

Volume 4

Volume 5

HIGGINS & HAWKE MYSTERY SERIES (cozy 1930s historical)

The 1930s meets Rizzoli & Isles in this friendship depression era cozy mystery series.

Death at the Tavern

Death on the Tower

Death on Hanover

Death by Dancing

THE ROSA REED MYSTERIES

(1950s cozy historical)

Murder at High Tide

Murder on the Boardwalk

Murder at the Bomb Shelter

Murder on Location

Murder and Rock 'n Roll

Murder at the Races

Murder at the Dude Ranch

Murder in London

Murder at the Fiesta

Murder at the Weddings

A NURSERY RHYME MYSTERY
SERIES (mystery/sci fi)

Marlow finds himself teamed up with intelligent and savvy Sage Farrell, a girl so far out of his league he feels blinded in her presence - literally - damned glasses! Together they work to find the identity of @gingerbreadman. Can they stop the killer before he strikes again?

Gingerbread Man

Life Is but a Dream

Hickory Dickory Dock

Twinkle Little Star

LIGHT & LOVE (sweet romance)

Set in the dazzling charm of Europe, follow Katja, Gabriella, Eva, Anna and Belle as they find strength, hope and love.

Love Song

Your Love is Sweet

In Light of Us

Lying in Starlight

PLAYING WITH MATCHES (WW2 history/romance)

A sobering but hopeful journey about how one young German boy copes with the war and propaganda. Based on true events.

A Piece of Blue String (companion short story)

THE CLOCKWISE COLLECTION (YA time travel romance)

Casey Donovan has issues: hair, height and uncontrollable trips to the 19th century! And now this ~ she's accidentally taken Nate Mackenzie, the cutest boy in the school, back in time. Awkward.

Clockwise

Clockwiser

Like Clockwork

Counter Clockwise

Clockwork Crazy

Clocked (companion novella)

Standalones

Seaweed

Love, Tink

ACKNOWLEDGMENTS

Many thanks to all the people who pull together to bring a new book baby into the world. My beta readers Angelika Offenwanger and Wendy Squire, my cover designer Steven Novak, my editor Marie Jaskulka and all my online writer friends (seriously couldn't do this without my writing community). A big squeeze to my moral support system of my husband Norm Strauss, my kids, my parents, and friends, especially Lori, Donna, Shawn, Norine and Marie.

Special thanks to Monica Pullman who won my "name a character in my book contest" and gave me the wonderful name of Artimisha.

All my blogger and social media fans, and especially YOU, for reading one of my books and making it to the acknowledgment page – Thank you!

As always, love and thanks to Jesus, the giver of peace.